NOT MY FAULT

Behind the Scenes
Book 2

SHANNON OCONNOR

Content Warnings

Please note some of these might be considered spoilers for parts of the story.

- PCOS (Poly cystic ovarian syndrome)
on page representation

- Recreational Marijuana / Marijuana Edibles use
on page representation

- Misgendering of a Nonbinary Main Character
on page representation

NOT MY FAULT

Playlist

Not My Fault (With Megan Thee Stallion) - Renee Rapp

Too Well - Renee Rapp

She's Pretty - Beth McCarthy

Something To Talk About - Bonnie Raitt

Pretty Girls - Renee Rapp

Talk Too Much - Renee Rapp

Bruises - Renee Rapp

Hurting My Own Feelings - Beth McCarthy

Oh Shit...are we in love? - Valley

Cure - Valley

Sorry I'm Here For Someone Else - Benson Boone

We Are Never Ever Getting Back Together (Taylor's Version) - Taylor Swift

Sucker - Jonas Brothers

Sexual Vibe - Stephen Puth

Play With Fire - Tessa Violet

To Renee Rapp

" Can a gay girl get an amen?"
- Renee Rapp

ONE

Emily

Someone tosses a pink bra at my head that I manage to duck at the last second.

"Hey! If you hit me, we might have to stop the concert. Be careful with your aim." I laugh. It's not the first time this has happened to me.

"How's everyone doing tonight?!" I shout into the bedazzled, pink microphone.

The crowd goes wild like it always does, and I smile. It's a bigger crowd than usual, but my agent said we sold out tonight. That is starting to happen more and more. I glance among the crowd, looking at the room filled with mostly women and non-binaries and a few token men. It makes sense; I have a habit of taking my top off for the ladies, and I do sing about loving women. It makes me feel more relaxed knowing who is out there. As the lights change throughout the night, it's harder to see exactly who's who, but in the beginning, I always get a vibe for the crowd.

"I think I'm going to start with an old favorite!" I announce and the crowd cheers as the band behind me plays the music to my number one hit.

I turn around, shaking my ass at the crowd, and start singing.

I've practiced this all week, so I know it like the back of my hand. This song is always a crowd pleaser and the perfect way to pump them up for the night. I dance around the stage, shaking my ass and grinding on my backup dancers like we practiced. I lean in during the chorus to almost kiss one of them, then pull away at the last second, making the fans scream even louder.

It's addictive; it makes my heart flutter in anticipation of more. I can never get enough of an adoring crowd. I'm an attention whore and I love it, but only like this. I can do without the crazy fans trying to break into my apartment or the paparazzi tracking me down. But the crowd going wild and cheering my name? That is what makes all that other stuff worth it.

I drop low and shake my ass one last time before the song ends and eat up the crowd. People are throwing stuff onto the stage, and I laugh as I dodge another bra. The music behind me starts and I kick into the next song. I need to stay on track with timing or Viv, my agent/manager, will have my ass. It costs way too much to go overtime with everything. Stage right, my bestie Georgiana (Georgie) is singing along with the song and I smile. She's supported me from the beginning, when I was writing songs in my journal and kissing straight girls who only wanted to experiment. She is my ride or die and spends most nights watching the concert live, when she isn't at her own job.

The band behind me hasn't been with me from the start, but I'd fight if Viv or anyone tried to switch them out on me. They're all a part of the Alphabet Mafia, each of them being talented on their instruments. Ella is on the drums, the baby of the band. Chrissy and Dana play guitar, along with Ty, who plays keyboard. I love having such a diverse group on stage with me. It makes being up here more fun than when it was just strangers in the beginning. It took a while of swapping out a person here or there to finally make the band what it is today.

I stop during one of Chrissy and Dana's guitar solos to grab some water. Someone backstage hands it to me, and I take a large chug then dump the rest of it on me. I am sweating. With the lights and all the dancing, it is impossible not to be. Just as they're finishing, I jump back on stage with my now wet white T-shirt.

"Who wants me to take it off?!" I shout as the crowd starts to cheer my stage name, LULY.

I put the mic between my thighs and seductively take off my T-shirt. I'm wearing a bright pink bralette under just for this reason. I love taking my clothes off on stage; something about it is invigorating and powerful. It is one of Viv's least favorite things I do, but she isn't always in charge. I can feel her scowl on me from stage left. The crowd goes wild. I lift my top to flash them, and they go even crazier. I laugh, fix my bralette, toss my T-shirt into the crowd, and watch the fans go rabid for it. I have to admit, it's pretty hot.

"I have one last song for tonight: how do we feel New York City?!" I shout, giving them a hint to singing an old favorite. It is my least favorite to sing but it is a crowd favorite and a crowd pleaser, so I always lose this debate.

I start singing, dancing with the band and touching the hands of the crowd in the front. People are touching my boots, and I eat it up. It is wild how far we've come since I started. I want to soak up every last second of this. As the song ends, I take a bow and then give the band a chance to have their own moment in the spotlight. I'm not some diva who can't give everyone a second in the light. I run off stage right to meet Georgina, who greets me with a hug and a bottle of water.

"You're all sweaty!" She giggles.

"Don't act like you don't love it!" I laugh.

We're both escorted further backstage, where Viv and other people on the team are waiting for me. Every night after the concerts, Viv tells me what I need to fix for the next performance. But tonight is bigger than that; we've been waiting to see who will be headlining Coachella this year. I'm supposedly a shoo-in, but I'm still nervous. I've had sold out shows for weeks, but this is *Coachella*. It's a huge honor.

"Emily, darling." Viv smiles. "Georgie, why don't you grab yourself a snack while we chat?" She's always trying to drive a wedge between us, but I don't budge.

"Georgie stays, Viv. Just tell me." I hold Georgie's hand tighter.

"Unfortunately, Coachella decided to go a different way this year." Her mouth forms a straight line. My shoulders slump and I sigh; I knew I shouldn't have gotten my hopes up.

"Okay."

"But great show! I'll give you my notes later. Have fun and get some rest before tomorrow." Viv squeezes my shoulder gently before leaving Georgie and I alone.

"I'm so sorry." Georgie frowns.

I slump into the couch and kick off my shoes. "I just thought this was my year."

"I know, but it's not like you'll never get it. It's just not your time yet."

I nod, unsure of what else to say.

"Why don't we head home and grab some gluten-free pizza from that place you love on Smith Street? I can have it delivered by the time we get to our apartment," she suggests.

"Only if you also get some buffalo wings and the gluten-free Mac," I tell her.

"Of course." She laughs.

I get up, changing into a pair of sweats and a crop top, sans bra. I know I'm about to be hoarded by the paparazzi, but it isn't like I need to look like a top model. I wipe off most of the makeup I'm wearing and look for my phone. It's probably in the safe, so I unlock it and grab my things. Georgie taps away on her phone, probably ordering food, and follows me out. Security walks us through the door and toward the SUV. I would've preferred to take the subway, but it's safer this way. With more popularity comes more recognition.

"LULY! LULY!"

"LOOK THIS WAY LULY!"

"SMILE!"

"ARE YOU UPSET ABOUT MISSING COACHELLA?"

I stop short in my tracks. How the hell does anyone know about that already. The flash of photography in all directions should blind me, but I'm wearing my extra dark shades for this purpose. Catching my response, the guy tries again.

"I TAKE IT YOU HEARD YOU WERE DENIED COACHELLA FOR A MORE TALENTED SINGER? SUCKS YOU CAN'T PLAY!"

"SHOW US YOUR TITS!"

"LULY! LULY!"

"You wanna see 'em?" I don't know what comes over me, but I use my free hand to lift my crop top and show my tits. I spin around, making sure everyone gets a good look and throw up the middle finger as well.

"Are you serious? Em, you know better than to do that!" Georgie scolds me when I get in the car. Sometimes she's more of a mom to me than my own mother is. She loves telling me to take it easy.

"What? Did you not get a good enough look? I can show you again if you like." I wink and she blushes, turning red as a tomato even though she's the straightest woman I know. If you can't act gay with your bestie, then who can you be gay with?

"You know Viv said to be careful. I'm just looking out for you."

I take her hand and squeeze it gently. "I know, and I appreciate it. It's not like it's anything I haven't done or shown before."

The driver drops us off at our apartment, which is one of the securest buildings in the city. I had to move several months ago after things started to pick up, and I wasn't leaving my best friend behind on the lease. We've always shared an apartment, both of us moving here almost seven years ago. We've gone from a studio apartment we shared to this, which is a penthouse apartment overlooking Central Park. I think we've done pretty well for ourselves. Georgie's successful on Wall Street, so even though she doesn't have to, she chips in on the rent every. She grabs the food, and we head into the apartment. All I want to do is relax with my bestie and maybe take an edible in the bath after.

"Are you fucking kidding me?!" Viv shouts the second she walks into my apartment. It's way too fucking early for her. Maybe I shouldn't have had that second gummy last night but one never seems to be working until I take another.

"What the hell are you shouting about?" I look down and realize I'm not wearing any pants, but hell if she hadn't bombed my phone with calls until I let her in. I didn't think she'd be bringing along two of her assistants. They stand behind her feebly, terrified her rage might turn to them.

"Is everything okay?" Georgie comes out rubbing her eyes, but at least she's wearing pants and a robe.

"No. You want to explain this?" Viv smacks down a newspaper on the kitchen island.

"Uh, you still buy newspapers? I didn't know they made those everyday anymore," I muse with a yawn.

"This is why you didn't get Coachella," she says sharply, waking me up quicker than a cup of coffee.

"What? But this just came out; they decided about Coachella already."

"You didn't get it because you're always being wild, showing your tits or flipping off the paparazzi." She scoffs.

"What the hell did you expect? My slogan is literally 'Great tits, bigger heart'."

"You need to calm down. I can't keep doing damage control if you're always going wild. I can only salvage so much, Emily."

"I think you're overreacting." I sigh. We have this fight at least once a month.

"Coachella reached out today and gave this as an example of why they didn't pick you." She sighs. Viv holds out her hand and one of the assistants— don't know their names because she always has new ones—gives her a phone, and Viv shows me the email from Coachella.

I read it in my head, biting on the inside of my cheek. Fuck. Is she right? I didn't think I was that bad. Am I?

TWO

Gus

I step back into the tattoo shop, and River gives me a weird look. "I thought you were going out for lunch?"

"My plans got cancelled." I try not to show how annoyed I am about that. Cari had cancelled them as I was walking out the door, which is a huge pet peeve of mine.

"Oh damn, I'm sorry." River frowns. It isn't like she knew I was going to have an afternoon hookup with her best friend. At least I don't think she knew.

"It's all good, I'm gonna grab a power bar, and then I can take some walk-ins." I shrug and head toward the back of the shop.

Isla and Rae are in their respective offices tattooing clients, while River is manning the front. We really should hire someone to cover the desk, but it's been on our to do list for longer than I care to admit. We don't mind doing everything ourselves—in fact, I think we sort of prefer it that way. I grab a peanut butter chocolate protein bar from the cabinet in the kitchen/break room and head back to my office. I pull out my phone and lounge in my client chair to relax for a few. My back is killing me today, and I want to rest it a bit before I have another client.

Cari and I are doing this thing where we hookup and hang out, but she isn't ready to commit yet. She's been burned badly in the past and is hesitant to get into anything serious. I get that; it isn't my favorite thing but I like her and am willing to wait. I just don't love that while we aren't serious, she's seeing other people. Or really, just one person in particular. And I'd probably like Max if this wasn't the way we met. River got married a few months ago after rekindling with her ex, Aspen. Aspen and River introduced Cari and Max first and I'm not so sure what happened, but they've been hot and cold for a while. On one of the 'cold' times, Cari and I hooked up. I'm not so into one-night stands, and I always thought she was gorgeous. What threw me for a loop was the fact that it's been over six months and she's still not ready to commit to one of us.

I leave Cari's text on read and grumble to myself. If she wasn't so freaking perfect, I'd be more upset with her. I love hanging out with her, even when we aren't hooking up. So call me a simp, but I'm hoping one day she'll end things with Max for good and stick with me.

Crumbling up the granola bar wrapper, I toss it in the garbage and then wash my hands. I poke my head down the hall and see a few more people waiting on the couches. River's talking to someone at the desk and the rest seem to be waiting, so I decide to see if I can help any of them.

"Hey, anyone here for a walk-in?" I ask.

Two guys and two girls stand together, and the girls push the guys to go first. They all walk over to me behind the desk on the opposite side of River. I notice they're all dressed in black from head to toe—the girls wearing black dresses and the guys wearing black button downs and nice pants. Did they just come from a funeral or something?

"I'm Gus, how can I help you?"

"We'd all love to get a tattoo, but we don't know how much it will be or, like, how long this takes?" The man in front speaks;

he's got a deeper voice than I anticipate. His shaggy, dark brown hair is in a mess around his face.

"Do you have an idea on the size or what the tattoo is?" I ask, opening the laptop we use to make sales.

"Yeah, we each want a slice of pizza that if near each other makes a full pie," the girl says, showing me a Pinterest photo of their idea. It's not uncommon; we get a lot of people coming in with ideas from Pinterest.

"So, I would have to draw this myself as that's another artist's design, but I can definitely do it. Are we looking for one inch? Maybe two?" I hold up my fingers to show the difference between one and two.

The group looks at each other and then nod, the first guy talking again, "Two please."

"Okay, it would probably be about twenty minutes for each of you, and we have a shop minimum of $85 per tattoo."

"That's perfect," the blonde girl says.

"Do we have enough time?" the redheaded girl asks.

"We're fine on time. Don't worry," the guy reassures her and rubs her shoulder gently.

"Okay, I need you each to fill out this form, back and front, and I need your IDs to verify age. Does anyone have any allergies?" I ask.

"Does gluten count?" the blonde asks shyly.

"No, but it doesn't hurt to mention."

She nods, and they each take turns filling out the forms and hand me their IDs. The two men share the same last name but the girls don't. I can't figure out their group dynamic. Are they couples or siblings? I guess it doesn't really matter, but I'm curious by nature. I finish signing them in and draw a quick sketch on the iPad nearby. The girls and I were always swapping iPads with whoever is nearby. We each have our own, of course, but sometimes it is easier to grab what is closest. I make sure the sketches look good to everyone and print it out on the tattoo transfer paper.

"I can take you all back if you're okay hanging out in the hall. Only two people fit with me tattooing," I explain.

"That works," the guy says.

They follow me to the room, and I begin setting up for the first tattoo. I double check if they need color, but they all want it in black ink. One of the guys takes a seat first after they do rock, paper, scissors to see who goes first. I don't see any visible tattoos on any of them, so I think it's safe to assume this is their first tattoo.

"Remind me your name?" I ask.

"I'm Taylor." The guy smiles.

"Okay, Taylor, I'm going to shave your arm then place the stencil. If you like it then I'm good to start tattooing."

"Sounds good." He looks a little nervous, but he nods. His… *company* looks on as I start the process.

"I can't believe we're doing this," the blonde girl mumbles.

"We promised we would," the other guy says.

"I know but being here makes it even more real." The other girl looks around the room nervously.

"We're getting this as a tribute to a friend of ours who died," Taylor explains as I begin to tattoo.

"I'm so sorry."

"Yeah, she was sort of wild and brought us all together as friends. And when she got sick, we promised we'd get a tattoo to remember her," Taylor adds.

"We hoped we wouldn't have to, none of us like needles," the blonde says.

"I'm sure she appreciates the sentiment," I say.

"We're on our way to her funeral after this," the redhead adds.

"We thought it would be a good way to get some closure," The other guy says.

They each have tears in their eyes as I finish tattooing their friend. I've done my fair share of memorial tattoos in my life, so this is nothing new. A lot of people don't realize how cathartic it is to get a tattoo. People like to use it as a therapy of sorts, and it often helps with healing. I've seen people commemorate all sorts of things and people on their bodies.

I move on from friend to friend, the last two holding hands as the redhead is tattooed. She squeezes her eyes shut and tries not to squirm. The blonde coaxes her through it, telling her it'll be okay, and I'm almost done. When the tattoo is all done, she opens one eye slowly and then the other.

"Oh my God," she says, and I freeze, waiting for the next words. I've only had a few people in my chair over the years really regret the tattoo they got.

"What?" the blonde asks.

"I can't believe she's gone." The girl starts to cry as she looks at her tattoo, and I hand her a box of tissues. She takes one, blows into it as hard as she can, and sobs louder.

"Dude, you're going to fill the room with tears. Save some for the funeral," Taylor says jokingly.

"I'm sorry." The blonde gives me a solemn look.

"No worries, I'll step out and give you a moment. Feel free to come up when you're ready." I clean up the important things quickly and leave the rest for when I come back, tossing my gloves in the garbage and heading toward the front.

"Everything okay? Didn't you have clients?" River looks at me as I come out alone.

"They're having a moment. It was a memorial tattoo," I explain.

She nods and I take a sip of water. Everyone already paid, so all I need to do is give them their aftercare card/goodie bag. It has a small bottle of soap, some stickers with our logo, a business card, and a card with the aftercare instructions. I place four of them on the counter and tilt my head down the hall to check on them but they're walking toward me.

"All good?" I check.

"Yes, thank you for everything," the blonde says.

"Here are some aftercare goodie bags. Please read the instructions and do the aftercare or they could get infected," I explain.

"Got it." Taylor nods.

They head out the door and down the stairs. The shop is empty right now, which wasn't uncommon. It's mid-day, and unless it's the weekend, we don't get too many walk-ins at this time. River's cleaning the front desk, and I think about asking her about Cari to see what kind of vibes she's giving her about me. But I think the better of it. I really don't want to put River in the middle of anything.

"You okay? You seem antsy." River raises an eyebrow at me.

"Eh, just nervous energy, I guess. How's Aspen doing?" I know changing the subject to her wife will take the attention off me.

"She's good. We're thinking about moving out of my apartment and finding something together. But of course, trying to find a place right now is kind of hell. So we will wait and see." She shrugs.

"I'll keep an ear out if I hear anything. Are you looking for anything in particular?"

"Not really. Close to work would be nice. But otherwise, we're fine with one or two bedrooms," River says.

"Got it." I nod.

My attention drifts to my phone buzzing in my pocket.

Cari: I'm so sorry I had to cancel

    Cari: I fell so behind on editing the last few days

    Cari: Can I see you tonight?

    Cari: I promise to make it up to you 😈

I smirk; she knows exactly how to get me back. I hate that I'm so far gone for her. As much as I want to deny it, I'll be back in her bed later tonight for sure. It isn't like she is doing anything wrong. She's been up front about everything—even offered details if I wanted them, which I don't. I think it is more the fact that I know she isn't having an open relationship to be with anyone, she's having it to be with Max. And if I had to guess, that is the reason she fell behind on editing. Sighing, I start typing a text back.

Me: What time can I come over?

THREE

Emily

"I think we should be doing damage control on your image," Viv continues, like she hasn't rocked my world by showing me that email.

"How?" Georgie chimes in.

"We have a plan to make you look more…approachable and tame by media standards," one of the assistants chimes in.

"I need pants for this. Have a seat and I'll be right back." I sigh.

I reach my bedroom and grab a pair of shorts. This is not at all how I wanted to wake up or spend the morning. Sighing, I grab my phone and head back for the kitchen. Everyone is sitting around my dining room table while Georgie and one of the assistants are making coffee. She knows she doesn't have to do that, but I also know she likes helping when she can't do anything else. I sit at the head of the table and Georgie brings me my coffee in my favorite mug. It's pink, has a picture of a middle finger, and says *don't fuck with me before coffee*. Viv frowns as I hold up the cup and drink a hearty sip.

Viv is usually frowning. I'm not quite sure what she likes about this job or if she's ever truly enjoyed it. She's older than my parents, probably in her sixties, with more wrinkles from the constant frowning. Her hair is always in a perfect bob, straightened to align her high cheek bones and sharp jaw. Her lips are a bare pink with no lipstick, and she has little to no makeup. She's usually wearing a suit or something professional. I always wonder how she got into this line of work, but it isn't something she talks about often.

"Let's get started, shall we?" she says in a sharp voice.

"Georgie, come join us," I tell her. I want her to hear all of this too.

"We have you scheduled for several talk show appearances over the next few months that you will have to prepare for," the assistant says.

"I know how to do an interview—" I start.

"You'll need to be prepped about what you should and should not be discussing. We're trying to tame your image; we can't afford you going rogue right now." Viv sighs.

"Fine, what else?" I know better than to push anything right now. I can pick my battles later.

"We booked you on Sesame Street in a few weeks—"

This time I'm the one to cut them off. "Are you serious?" I say with a laugh.

"You'll be the musical guest and they're adapting one of your songs to fit the show," they continue.

"It shows you care about children and can keep your shirt on, which a lot of people aren't sure of right now. Plus, the parents watching will have face recognition which is good for your brand."

"Okay." I just nod.

"The last thing is a little more complicated…" The assistant passes the folder to Viv, and she looks it over before sighing.

"The media has a lot of speculations about you and your romantic life. Especially since you are often seen with different women and have never been in a long-term relationship, according to them."

"Okay? So you want me to talk about my dating life or something?"

"We want you to find someone to be in a relationship with. Either a real one or one for PR. There are several women we could recommend and set you up with in a mutually beneficial contract, or if there's someone in your life that you'd be willing to date publicly…" Viv's eyes fall to Georgie, whose eyes widen, and I step in.

"Absolutely not! I've said this time and time again. Georgie is my straight best friend. There's nothing going on between us, real or otherwise. I will not have her thrown into the spotlight just so it looks good for me." I shake my head.

"Okay, then are you willing to be set up?"

"I'm too busy to have a real relationship, how would I have time to promote a fake one?"

"Well, we'd be doing that for you. You'd have to make sure to be photographed a few times here and there with the person but otherwise we'd be the ones spinning the narrative."

"So I'd have a fake girlfriend I don't even know and I wouldn't be able to go out and get laid without looking like I'm cheating on said girlfriend?" I realize.

"Well, yes. You'd have to agree to a term of a no cheating clause. Behind closed doors is fine but if you were caught with someone else it would completely destroy the purpose," they continue.

So I'm not allowed to have a social life anymore? I'm already severely limited on where I can go and when, but now I'm not even allowed to sleep with who I want? Unless they signed some NDA? This is insane. I can feel the rage bubbling up inside me, but before I can say anything, Georgie grabs my hand and squeezes it.

"Do you think we could have some time to look everything over? Surely you don't want Emily rushing into anything without thinking it through?" Georgie speaks softly, and Viv's face changes from annoyed to neutral.

"Yes, I suppose that's fine." She's clearly biting back saying more but Georgie has some good points.

"You can leave the paperwork with me, and I'll make sure we look it over." Georgie adds.

Viv and her assistants leave without another word, and I sigh in relief. Thank God I have Georgie here to help me fight my battles. I truly don't know what I'd do without her.

"I know this seems like a lot, and you looked like you were going to scream, so I figured it was best we talked it over ourselves," Georgie explains.

"Thank you. I just can't imagine being with someone for events and all that bullshit and not being able to go out and be myself."

"It's not preventing you from being yourself, they just want you to show the media you aren't a wild child corrupting their children. Celebrities all over the place do stuff like this all the time. You can afford a few months without your wild child tendencies," she says.

"What if I don't want to?"

"Then don't. You know I always have your back. But I have to say, they might have the right to drop you as a client if you're not adhering to certain clauses such as morality or fitting the image they expected."

"I hate it when you get all lawyery on me." I roll my eyes.

"Hey, I have to put my one semester of law school to good use sometimes." She laughs. She started law school, stayed one semester, and decided it wasn't right for her. But her small bouts of legal knowledge do come in handy every once in a while.

"Where would I even find someone to fake date?"

"They did put together a list but after looking it over, I doubt you'd want to see any of them."

"Who are they?" I asked, my curiosity piqued.

"Mostly influencers, a lot of them promoting healthy lifestyles and easy-going lives."

"I do not want to be connected to an influencer. No fucking way."

"I know. I'm just saying these are the ones that believe some of the same things you do. It might not hurt to at least meet some of them and see how it goes." Georgie shrugs.

I stand up from the table and place my now-empty coffee mug into the sink. I reach for some gluten-free waffles and the low-sugar syrup. It doesn't taste as good as the high sugary, high gluten stuff, but it helps with my PCOS symptoms. When my doctor recommended going gluten free to combat my tiredness, I thought she was nuts. But here I am a year later, having more energy than I've ever had in my life and it's because of the lack of gluten in my diet. I pop the waffles in the toaster and wait for them to brown; I liked them nice and crunchy.

"What if you just met up with them? No one is saying you have to pick them or be with them. But it shows Viv and your label that you're willing to try and work with them," Georgie offers.

"Do I have to meet up with all of them?" I grimace as I put the hot waffles on a plate and pour a small amount of syrup over them.

"No, well…What if you like, speed dated them? You can see what each one has to offer and then say no."

"Fine. I actually like that idea. I'll let Viv know." I sigh.

"I know this isn't what you want, but if you let them do this, then you can focus on what you want. Which we both know is singing." Georgie joins me on the couch.

"You're right. I just haven't touched my song book in months, and the label is on my back to write for the new album, but it's hard when I have no spare moments. Now I'm going to have even less to fix something that isn't broken?"

"Who knows, maybe you'll end up meeting the love of your life," Georgie teases.

"You've been reading too many of those romance novels." I shake my head.

"Fake dating to lovers is one of the most common tropes. All that pretending blurs the lines and people don't know how to feel." She shrugs with a smile.

"So why aren't you out fake dating someone?"

"I'm trying. If you meet a man I'd like, send them my way." She groans.

Songwriting used to come so easily to me. I'd have a thought or a feeling and the words would flow. But now, with the anticipation of it being picked apart by fans and the label, it's daunting. I don't want people to think I'm a one-album wonder, but I also don't want my second album to flop. I know I need to get out of my head about it, but that's easier said than done.

Maybe once everything is taken care of with this stuff, I'll have a better handle on where to start. It doesn't help that I'm constantly working or thinking about working. I don't have time to eat some days, let alone think. I don't know what I'm feeling because I never have the chance to ponder it for more than a moment. At least I made time this week to get a new tattoo. If I didn't schedule that like, weeks in advance, it would never happen. It's my me-time and almost a therapy session where I felt like I can breathe again.

My tattoo artist, River, and I met almost a year ago when she reached out begging for me to play her girlfriend's birthday party. It was such a sweet sentiment that I never got, and I knew I had to say yes. And I'm glad that I did. She's a talented artist, and we've kept in touch since. She did a tattoo of the middle finger by my hip bone that came out adorable. This time I'm going for a much bigger chest piece, and I know she's going to knock it out of the park. She sent me sketches and I'm already in love. Hopefully it won't hurt as much as I think it will. I can handle the pain okay, but it would be a lot longer of a session than before. I have to go after-hours so no one will recognize me either.

I decide to text Viv that I'm in for meeting the influencers she thinks would be a good match. She texts back immediately, telling me I won't regret it. But suddenly I have a huge knot in my stomach.

FOUR

Gus

"If you kiss me like that again, I'm going to be late for my meeting." Cari blushes as I kiss her neck. Her blonde curls are a mess from last night, but I can't keep my lips off her.

"So? Skip it." I don't know who I am, because I am never someone to consider skipping work.

"I can't." She moans softly as I bite her earlobe. "Fuck, *Gus*."

"We could spend the whole day in bed, or on other surfaces..." I stop talking to kiss down her cheek in a line for her pink, pouty lips.

"I wish I could, but this is an important meeting." She sighs and gets off the bed.

I fall into her pillows and look up at her as she shakes out her hair and pulls it into a bun. Cari saunters around the room naked, her curves and body on display. She's confident in everything she does, which is what drew me to her. She finds a dress to wear and places the hanger on the back of her door. She ties a silk blue robe around her waist and looks back at me.

"I don't want to kick you out, but I do have to shower before this meeting." She looks at me with her big blue eyes.

"What if we shower together?"

"I wish, but I'm running late since someone didn't remind me to set the alarm," she teases.

"Okay, what about tonight? We could go see that new scary movie you wanted to watch?" I suggest.

Her face twists; it's subtle. The curl of her lip and the way her eyebrows narrow, just before changing into a neutral expression.

"I can't tonight, I'm seeing—"

I cut her off. "Got it."

Cari sighs and I know I've probably said the wrong thing, but I hate knowing she's going out with Max. I'm jealous as can be, and it's stupid because I have no right to be. I just don't have it in me to fight her on it and demand more. If she wants more, I want it to be her idea, not something that's forced upon her. I grab my clothes from the floor and start getting dressed.

"Babe, don't do this." She tilts her head down and bats her dark eyelashes at me.

"I'll see you, okay?" I kiss her forehead and head for the front door.

I'm not someone who cries, but damn do I want to punch something right now. Standing in the elevator, looking at my own reflection, I think about punching myself. I'm in my thirties, for God's sake. What the hell am I doing with someone who doesn't want the things I want. I know better than this. Clenching my fists, I storm out the building and head downtown to my apartment. I don't have work today so I may as well go home and get some sleep. Maybe I'll hit the gym in my building and get a workout in to alleviate this anger.

On my way out the door, I feel my phone buzz in my pocket. I'm positive it's Cari texting or calling to apologize. But I don't bother looking. I'm not in the mood to see what she has to say. So I head for the 6 train downtown. I live in Bushwick. I grew up just outside of New York, in a small town in New Jersey, but as soon as I was old enough, I grabbed the first train to the city. My dad always said my personality was too big for a small town; I don't think he's wrong. But it's more than that. Being non-binary isn't easy for anyone in a small and close-minded town. Here, I'm able to dress and look how I want. Sure, most days that's more masculine-leaning, but it isn't like I have someone telling me I need to look a certain way.

I swipe my stupid OMNY card on the reader before sliding through the turnstile and heading to the train. I miss my Metro-Card; I had waited as long as humanly possible to switch to this stupid thing. I'm nostalgic and stubborn, I guess, but the new card doesn't hit the same way a MetroCard always did. The new card feels like a credit card, but it scans you though. Gone is my swipe that may or may not go through.

I pop in my AirPods as I take a seat on the train. It's just after eleven, so it isn't crowded. Everyone who needs to go to work is already there, and anyone else is a tourist looking for the Brooklyn Bridge or a local heading home. I know how many songs it takes to get home once I'm on the train so I can mostly tune out. Tapping my foot along to the song, I relax a bit. I won't admit this out loud, but I'm obsessed with that new singer, LULY. After hearing her play live at Aspen's birthday party, I saved all her songs to my Spotify. Most of them are poppy and upbeat, but there are a few from some EPs that are more toned down. She stripped down her emotions and bared her soul on those tracks. I was impressed. These are the songs that I listen to when I want to feel something. Not that I won't put on some of her happier tracks when I'm in the mood to get hype. Or if I'm going out drinking.

Not that it happens much anymore. Most of my friends have settled down with a partner and kids, leaving me to the bars. It's better than dating apps, but not by much. It isn't that I don't like going out, but I definitely don't like the one-night stand expectations. Or the fact that bars seem to be so loud lately it's like you can't have a conversation in them.

My best friend, Kenzie, had it easy with her wife, Barbie. They've been married for years now and travel all the time for both of their careers. Barbie is the CEO of a successful toy company, and Kenzie is a successful plus-size model. They had a complicated relationship that was five years of loss of contact followed by them falling back in love. I don't have anyone I'd want to fall *back* in love with, but I wouldn't mind falling in love for the first time. In some ways, I'm jealous. I don't know if I necessarily want a wife and kids one day, but a long-term partner? Someone to wake up with every morning? That sounds like heaven to me.

By the time I'm back to my apartment, I'm relaxed enough that I don't feel like hitting the gym. I can always go later if I feel up for it. I unlock the door to my apartment and kick off my boots. All three of my cats come out of hiding to greet me.

"Hi Sparks, Bitsy, and Cat Burglar." I pick them each up and give them a kiss hello. They meow at me, and I put them back on the ground.

My neighbors' kids named them for me. I was struggling to pick names, and they insisted I name them after the cats on the show *SuperKitties*. The names have grown on me, and they work for them. I grab a fresh can of cat food from the kitchen cabinet and place it on the counter. They all walk to their bowls already on the floor and wait. I wash my hands to remove the grime from the subway, then open the can and give them a scoop. They aren't the biggest fans of the wet food, so I fill their bowls with some dry food too. Then I head into my room and get undressed.

I take off my chest binder and place it on my dresser. I don't love having my breasts free, but I don't want to potentially damage anything by wearing it too long. I'm home alone, so I put on a sports bra for some support. My breasts aren't big or anything, but they always feel like an attachment to me—one I don't know what to do with. I don't like the way they fit certain clothes, and I don't like the way men ogle at them. Sure, I like women too, but I hate being stared at like a piece of meat. That's the main reason I've chosen to wear binders when I'm out and about.

Bitsy jumps on my bed, and Sparks is not too far behind. I

adopted the three of them from a shelter nearby a few years after moving to the city. They are older now, almost eleven this year, and I don't want to google the lifespan of cats. Their different colored furs have started to gray but they are still going strong. Bitsy is a black cat while Sparks is black with some white spots, and Cat Burglar is an orange cat like Garfield. And yes, he's always getting into trouble, hence his silly name.

"I think I need a nap," I decide, looking at Sparks and Bitsy cuddling at the end of my bed.

I didn't get much sleep last night, and it isn't like I have much else to do. I have a load of laundry I can do, but I'm not up to it right now. Before climbing into bed, I put on a pair of boxer shorts and pick my phone out of my pants pocket. I ignore the messages from Cari and look at the missed texts from River. There are more than three, which worries me. I'm about to read them when I get an incoming call from her.

"River? What's up?" She doesn't typically call me on my day off. Or at all, for that matter.

"I'm so sorry to bother you, but I have to run to the hospital. Aspen sprained her freaking ankle at CrossFit. But I have a high-profile client coming in tonight and I really don't want to cancel on her. Is there any way you could come in later and take her?"

"Who's the client?"

"The singer from Aspen's birthday party, LULY. She wants a chest piece done."

"What time do you need me to come in?" I eye my very cozy looking bed. Maybe I won't be getting that nap after all.

"Just before close? She asked that the place is empty because of crazy fans, and since I thought I was doing it, I agreed."

"Okay, and what's the design like?"

"It's pretty general, nothing crazy or too much my style. Rae and Isla are already fully booked, and I'd hate to let someone else in town get the job." She sighs. River isn't my boss, so I could say no. But I also know how much a high-profile client like her would help the shop.

"Yeah, I can do it. Can you send me her contact info and the designs she wanted? And is Aspen going to be okay?"

"Thank you! Of course! Gus you're literally a lifesaver! And I think so, she's more upset than hurt, I think. She's never broken or sprained anything before, and I just want to be there for her. It sounds silly, I know—she's my wife, not a child—but still."

"No, I get it. You're worried and she needs you. You should absolutely be there for her," I reassure her.

River thanks me a million times over before hanging up. She sends over the email LULY/Emily sent to her and the art River was working on. I do a quick google search to remind myself who this is and what she looks like. I know the basics, and I know her music, but the last thing I want is to say something stupid in front of someone like her. River and I work on high-profile clients a lot, but it isn't usually people we recognized or people that make us starstruck. I hope that will be the case tonight. I slump into bed and decide to take a quick nap before I have to shower and head into work later.

Emily

"Hey, are you Gus?" I ask the masculine looking person behind the desk. River mentioned Gus uses they/them pronouns, so if it's them, I want to be sure to remember that.

"I am. You're Emily?" It seems like a question, which makes sense because to everyone in the world besides Georgie and Viv, I'm LULY.

"I am." I smile and shake their hand.

"River showed me what you're looking for, and I'm happy to do it, but she also said you can wait for her if you want. She apologizes for not being here."

"It's okay. I would normally wait, but I don't want to head into the summer with a fresh tattoo. I like swimming too much for that."

"Gotcha. Then have a seat. I've been drawing up the final plan and you can pick which one you like the best." They gesture to the couch behind me.

I fix my skirt and sit; they sit across from me on the chair and hold out an iPad open to Procreate. On it is a drawing of a beautiful chest piece. Roses and thorns arranged in a pattern that will fit between my tits.

"This is totally perfect."

"Awesome. If you want to head into my room down that way, I'll be right in." They point down the empty hallway and I nod.

Taking my purse with me, I plop it on the extra chair in the room. There's a wall of framed tattoo art and a few certificates claiming Gus is the winner of several tattooing competitions. I slide off my shades and put them in my bag. There's a mirror on the back of the door and I check my hair. I ditched the driver a few blocks away to walk. It's such a beautiful day out, and I knew it was crowded enough I wouldn't get caught. I wore a baseball cap and sunglasses like I'm Joe in an episode of YOU. Sure enough, no one saw me but now I have hat hair, so I quickly run my fingers through my blonde hair and slide on some fresh lip gloss.

River assured me that Gus is as professional and discrete as she is. But on the off-chance someone caught a photo of me, I want to look my best. Gus comes in a few minutes later and starts setting up the space to tattoo me. It isn't my first tattoo; River did my first six months ago. I mean, I have some of those stick and poke ones from when I was sixteen in someone's basement, but that doesn't count.

"You can have a seat; I'll have to lower you down into a laying position to do this. Is that okay?" Gus asks.

"Of course." I nod.

"It's a chest piece, right? Do you mind if I touch you?" Gus has on a pair of black rubber gloves but waits for confirmation from me.

"Go for it." I smile.

Gus looks at my chest, eyeballing where the tattoo will go. They slide my low-cut romper to the sides, not exposing me but seeing if they can put the tattoo paper on.

"It might be a little tricky with the fabric. If you're comfortable with it, we have tape and coverings so you can take off your shirt and still be covered."

"I think most of New York has seen my tits at this point, so I'm fine with whatever works for you." I laugh.

After I slide my romper sleeves down my arms, my breasts fall out, and Gus bites their bottom lip. I see the way their cheeks flush and their breathing hitches. Automatic responses for someone seeing a nice pair of tits. They quickly turn around and grab more supplies, handing them to me and standing.

"I'll step out and you can do that. Just tape and cover more toward your back than the middle." They aren't looking at me and I hold back a laugh.

"Okay." I nod.

Gus leaves the room, and I tape the girls to the sides. It's sort of like taping them up for a strapless dress. I sit back down on the chair, waiting for Gus to come back. When they do, after tapping lightly on the door, they seem more put together. More focused.

"So I just need to touch you to put on the tattoo stencil and then obviously I'll be working with you laying down. If you're uncomfortable at all or need a break, just let me know. Is there any music you'd like to listen to?" Gus asks.

"Is it okay if we don't have music? I kind of appreciate the quiet these days."

Gus smiles, all shiny white straight teeth. "Of course."

Gus picks up the stencil, places it over my chest, and adjusts before pressing it down to let the blue ink stain my skin. I look down, watching, not that I can really tell how the tattoo looks from this angle. They pick up a handheld mirror and hold it in front of me so I can see.

"It looks great." I nod.

They're sort of quiet, which I don't mind. I have too much on my plate right now, and I wasn't sure if I'd get someone who talked nonstop about what I do. River and I were chill, so I was nervous when I knew it wouldn't be her. She assured me Gus was just as professional and that's proving to be true. They tell me to lay back, and then they start setting up the tattoo gun and ink. Besides a few spots with shading, it's a lot of line work. I'll be here for a while, so I close my eyes and try to relax. As soon as the tattoo gun hits my skin, I tense up and try to remember what River told me. I don't want the tattoo looking weird because I'm tense, so I take in some deep breaths.

I wouldn't be so stressed if I hadn't let Georgie and Viv talk me into meeting the influencers they lined up to date me. It was a day from hell, and the only thing that got me through it was knowing I was getting tattooed tonight. It's like therapy for me. They set me up on what was essentially speed dating with seven women who had to sign NDAs just to show up. It was half-humiliating and half-exhausting. Each woman had their own set of flaws that I couldn't look over. One only showered every three days as a way of preserving their body's natural oils, one told me I would need to convert to being a Mormon if I ever wanted to meet her family, and another looked like she just rolled out of bed and didn't know where she was. How the hell were these women my only choices? I thought I was supposed to be showing the world a different side of me.

Viv explained these were successful influencers whose brand would help grow mine, but all I wanted to do was run out of there and take a shower. I hate the idea of being set up. It feels forced and unnatural. If I'm going to spend the better part of the next year with this woman, didn't I want it to be with someone I actually got along with? I let out an exasperated sigh.

"I'm sorry, did I hurt you?" Gus pulls back immediately.

"No! I'm sorry. I'm stressed thinking about work." I force a smile.

"You can talk about it if you like. I've been told I'm a good listener." They smile.

"Tattoo artists are the new bartenders? I should spill all my secrets?"

"Only if you want to." Gus goes back to tattooing and I take a moment to take them in.

They're attractive, obviously has a good job. River mentioned Gus was one of the owners, and this place is always busy when I want to swing by. Gus had cropped black hair and tattoos everywhere. I spot several on their arms, forming full sleeves, an array on their neck but not in a scary way—it sort of works for them—and they are wearing a thin silver chain around their neck. I usually go for more feminine people, but Gus is hot. I know I shouldn't be lusting over my tattoo artist, but it's like everyone I meet lately has turned into a potential subject.

"My boss is killing me. They're trying to set me up, and I feel like it's the 1800s and I'm being forced to marry a stranger for some cattle," I explain.

"Pretty sure it would take a lot more than one cow to marry you," Gus says. "I'm sorry, I was trying to make a joke, but I think that came out wrong."

I laugh. "It's okay. I'm working on changing my image, but it's hard when I'm not sure that I want to change. I just know I want to sing, but I can't sing without all the politics behind being in the limelight."

"You're a very talented singer."

"You've heard me sing?" I ask, surprised.

"Of course. You played Aspen's birthday last year, but I've been a fan since the beginning. Malibu Summer is one of my favorites," they say.

"No one ever says that. It's one of mine too." I smile.

Malibu Summer is one of my earlier songs, one of the ones I wrote and played before landing an agent and a steady gig. Not too many people even know it because it's not something I ever play live. Gus isn't just blowing smoke up my ass; they really were a fan.

"Your lyrics, they always speak to me. The pop ones are cool too, but the ones where you're almost crying singing them? They get me every time," Gus admits.

I'm in awe. Who is this person? No one ever talks to me

about music like this. Even real fans all want to know who My Summer Fling is about—one of my exes. They never want to discuss the deeper lyrics.

"The first three times I tried to record it, I was crying. I had to keep redoing it, but eventually I just left it in because I was out of studio time and I thought it felt more real with them in," I tell them.

"So powerful." Gus nods.

We continue talking about lyrics that have made a difference to us. All the singers we love and the venues around here. Gus is easy to talk to once they open up. They're quiet at first, but I think it's because they give space to everyone else to talk first. By the time my tattoo is finished, I'm bummed. I take out my phone and snap a few photos so I can see it better. Then I toss my phone aside and start taking off the wrappings. Gus covers my tattoo in that sticky tape-like stuff called second skin, and I throw the boob tape and wrapping into the garbage. They look away while I adjust my breasts and put my romper sleeves back on. I grab my hat and sunglasses, even though it's night, and put them back on.

"It's eleven hundred," Gus says as they ring me up out front. I hand them my credit card and reach in my wallet for cash. After handing Gus a one-hundred-dollar bill, they look at me, surprised.

"How much change do you need?"

"Oh no, that's your tip." I wave them off.

"Wow, thank you." They smile.

"I don't want to hurt River's feelings but if you're around next time, I wouldn't mind you doing my next tattoo as well." I smile.

"Of course, happy to help." They smile.

I head down the stairs, and just as I reach outside, Gus calls after me. They don't use my name, which I'm grateful for.

"Hey! You forgot this." Gus catches up to me and holds out my phone.

My eyes go wide. "You just saved my life! You have no idea. Thank you so much."

Without thinking about it, I pull Gus in for a tight hug. It stings a little when our chests bump together because of my tattoo, but it feels right. Gus blushes and I head down the block to find my driver.

Gus

Emily leaves and I head back inside to clean up the shop. It's getting late, and I want to get home before the rain starts tonight. Emily surprised me—she isn't some stuck up pop star, she's really kind and thoughtful. It surprised me when she hugged me, but in a good way. I know it will be a while before I see her again, but I'll be playing her music on the train ride home. I texted Cari earlier, but she still hasn't replied. She's probably too busy with Max to check her phone. I'm sure I'll get a text in a few days asking to see me, so until then, I just have to be patient.

Locking up the shop, I put on my headphones and turn on Emily's newest album. I grab my stupid non-MetroCard and head for the subway. I'll be home in twenty-two minutes as long as the train wasn't late. And the rain is set to start in thirty. I head down the stairs, through the turnstile, and check the screen for the latest updates. It's all black, which isn't uncommon. New York has a habit of putting up new screens and fixtures only for them to not work three months later and never get fixed again. It's a waste. I'm about to check my phone for the train time when I hear it coming. Two bright lights in a sea of darkness, the loud rumble and the vibration of the ground all at once. The train stops, I get on and take a seat along the side of the car. It's empty for this time of night, so I can relax.

It isn't something I think about often, but I don't like worrying about someone giving me a hard time on the train. Sometimes a transphobic person will think I'm trans and harass me for that, or other times I get people asking what I am. Both are rooted in ignorance, but it doesn't hurt any less. I make it home scot-free and head straight for bed. Well, I check on the cats first and give them cuddles before we all go to bed.

Before plugging in my phone, I pull up the tattoo shop's Instagram and upload Emily's tattoo. She said we could post it and tag her public account, which will help the shop grow. So I make sure to refer to her as LULY in the post and press upload before going to bed. I put my phone on the charger and fall asleep.

In the morning, I'm woken up to the sound of my phone alarm going off. Nine-thirty a.m. on my non-work days. Sparks meows at me, and after I stop to pee, I get them their breakfast. Returning to my room, I check my phone and my eyes snap open when I see hundreds of notifications. Most of them are from Instagram but a lot of them are also texts.

RIVER: I knew you had game but damn 👀 🔥

RAE: WHY DIDN'T YOU TELL US?!

ISLA: DON'T YOU LOVE US?! JK, but good job bro

· · ·

I'm so confused, I'm about to ask what the hell they're talking about when my best friend, Kenzie, texts me.

KENZIE: You're dating a lesbian icon, and this is how I have to find out?!

Attached to the text is a photo of a tabloid post that has a photo of Emily and I hugging outside the shop last night. I didn't even know there was paparazzi around, let alone that they caught us. But it isn't what it looks like. It was a friendly hug. Why was everyone freaking out about that? The headline says, LESBIAN SINGER CAUGHT HUGGING NEW BAE? Did people still use the word bae? Maybe they were trying to make sure not to mess up my pronouns. I keep reading.

Lesbian singer, LULY, was caught hugging unnamed partner outside local NYC tattoo shop, RARE's Tattoos. It is unknown if this is a new relationship or has been going on for a while. The couple seemed to be embracing before parting ways on the dark spring night.

Is this what passes for gossip these days? People are ready to believe anything they read, apparently, including my friends.

I text back the group chat with River, Rae, and Isla first.

ME: There is no tea, it was a friendly goodbye hug. She left her phone behind, I brought it to her, and she thanked me.
RIVER: We might have a little problem…

River attached a photo of all the DMs in the tattoo shop's account. Most of them wanted to be tattooed at the same place Emily was, or to be tattooed by me. A lot of them were referring to me as the 'hot' tattoo artist. I wasn't complaining about that, but I can't believe all this came from one little misunderstanding.

I guess it doesn't help that Emily reposted about her being tattooed by me last night. I have her number and could text her, but in case this hasn't reached her yet, I don't want it to be weird.

RAE: Can only say that I'm jealous

ISLA: Me too

ME: This is too much, I literally just hugged the woman. Nothing happened!

Then I text Kenzie back.

ME: There's more than meets the eye. I tattooed her yes, and we hugged, but that's all that happened.

KENZIE: I believe you, but only because you don't lie to me. However, the public won't believe it.

Sighing, I start to get ready for work. Between picking out clothes and taking a shower, I have to put my phone on silent because it keeps going off, and I can't keep checking it. I'm not one to enjoy the limelight. Like, I'm not opposed to it for the right reasons, but this all feels like a big misunderstanding. I get dressed, put a touch of gel in my hair, and head out for the day.

Even though I know it's crazy, I feel like people are watching me on the train. Like they recognize me and are trying to place where I'm from. Maybe it's in my head, but I swear I feel eyes on me. By the time I get to the studio, it's crowded outside, and I have to squeeze through a crowd to let myself in. A few people cheer when they see me, and my eyes widen as I head inside.

"What the hell's going on?" I say to River, noticing a tall security guard-looking man standing inside the doorway.

"This is one of Emily's bodyguards," River starts.

"She's in your office and wants to talk to you," Rae squeals.

"Okay…" I hesitate before heading for my office. I didn't think to stop for coffee today with everything going on, and I feel like I was going to need some caffeine for this.

"Hey," I say cautiously, opening the door.

"Gus, hey, I'm so sorry for just ambushing you at work, but I wanted to talk somewhere private." Emily's standing in my office with a brunette woman by her side. She looks familiar, like she's been photographed with her before or something. "Sorry, this is my best friend, Georgie."

"Hi, I'm Gus. Pleasure to meet you." I smile and shake her hand.

Georgie smiles and then we both look at Emily.

"I'm sorry about the photo. I didn't realize the paparazzi were around. I should've gone down first last night to protect you." I sigh.

"No! It's okay. It's actually why we're here. I wanted to ask you something."

"Okay?" I raise an eyebrow.

"My label is looking for me to date someone, for the media. Someone low key, down to earth, who won't take away attention from me, and keep my name out of the tabloids for the wrong reasons," Emily explains.

"Okay…" I still don't understand how I fit into this.

"Georgie and I were thinking, maybe that could be you…" she finishes with a smile.

"Excuse me, what?" My eyes go wide. Surely this was all a dream, and my alarm is about to go off any minute. I don't really have a pop star standing in my office asking me to be their fake girlfriend.

"We'd need you to sign an NDA and go out with me on a few fake public outings. But otherwise, you'd resume your normal life, and I would mine. The record company is offering a large check if you last six months, and more for a year," she explains.

"I'm sorry, I don't think I'm hearing you right. Are you asking me out?"

"No. I need someone to pretend to be my girlfriend—well partner. Whichever term you prefer. And to the press, we'd be a couple, but in private, we'd just be friends," Emily adds.

"Emily's label is worried about her image, and in the last twelve hours since your photo was taken, she's gone from being labeled the 'wild child' to a loyal lesbian. I know it's silly to have to worry about those things, but perception is everything, and we just want her to be able to focus on her music. This would be mutually beneficial to both of you," Georgie adds.

"So, we just have to look like we're dating? But we can date other people?" I think of Cari immediately.

"Well, no. You'd have to remain loyal to Emily, otherwise the press would have a field day with this." Georgie sighs.

"Which is why the label is willing to pay you. I know it's asking a lot." Emily does a half smile.

"I-I'm sort of seeing someone. Not seriously, but it could be. So I'm sorry but no. I just can't do this," I say aloud. Emily's face falls but she quickly adjusts it.

"I understand." She nods.

"You understand that even if you don't agree, this conversation needs to stay private?" Georgie adds.

"G, they're not going to tell anyone," Emily says before I can.

"She's right. Your secret is safe with me."

"Okay," Georgie says.

"I should get going then but thank you. If you happen to change your mind, you have my number. Just give me a call and

I can answer any questions if you're worried," Emily says before leaving.

I nod and watch as she walks down the hallway. The security guard opens the doors, and Emily takes the time to sign some things—which is a lot of boobs—and take photos with the fans. Before leaving, she turns back to give me a soft smile. I feel bad for saying no. I just don't want to miss my chance with Cari if I'm busy pretending to be with Emily.

"I know you probably can't tell us what happened, but can you check your phone? Cari asked me to tell you." River looks at me with an eyebrow raised.

Reaching into my pocket, I see a few missed texts from Cari. She's never one to double text, let alone triple or quadruple.

CARI: I know we said we could see other people, I didn't realize that included famous pop stars

CARI: I'm free tonight if you're not too busy

CARI: Okay, I saw your photo and maybe you're right. I'm not ready to be serious yet but I want to see you more

Is it possible that Cari is jealous of Emily? Is that why there's a sudden change in her? We've spent months doing the hot and cold dance, with most of it being cold. Until now, it seemed like she was leaning more for Max. Did I only have to take a photo with someone else? She thought she was losing me and now she wants to make sure that isn't the case. I'm flattered; maybe there is something to this thing with Emily. Nah, I text Cari back saying I can see her later and she responds right away.

SEVEN

Emily

Ever since I got my new tattoo, I've started writing in my song book again. It's like something about that day ignited something inside me. I know it's probably short-lived until I get another tattoo, but it's nice to be back to something familiar. I've carried my song book with me everywhere I go, just in case a lyric pops into my head. Of course, most of them had to do with being rejected.

Not that Gus rejected me, *not really*. They were already sort of seeing someone; I understand why they didn't want to risk ruining it with them to pretend to be with me. But it still hurts. I'm back to square one with no one to help. I thought that photo —and Gus—were the keys to my relationship problems, but I guess I was wrong. Part of me is still holding out hope they'll call me and say they changed their mind. But it's highly unlikely.

I have a podcast interview tomorrow, and one of the things I'll be asked about is that photo. I guess I'll be forced to tell the truth, that it was just me and my tattoo artist hugging. There's no secret romance going on, and I'm still as single as usual. I normally like being single, but not when Viv and my team are on my back to commit to someone. I don't want to miss out on furthering my career because I'm being deemed wild or challenging.

"Can we run it one more time?" I ask the backup dancers. They're back from break with fresh water and smiles. They nod just as Georgie runs toward me.

"G?" She normally knows better than to interrupt rehearsal.

"You got a text!" She pushes the phone toward me.

"I can answer it—"

She cuts me off. "It's *Gus*."

"Shit, sorry guys! I'll be right back. Give me five!" I take my phone, and Georgie follows me off the stage so I can call Gus back.

Of course they pick up on the first ring, "Hey!" I sound way too chipper.

"Hey, I hope it's okay I called."

"Of course, what's going on?" I ask, trying to sound casual.

"I was thinking about your...*offer*, and I think I'd like to discuss it further. Maybe talk about specifics before I agree," they say.

Georgie must hear Gus because her eyes go wide. "Yeah sure, I'm done with rehearsal in like an hour. Can I stop by the studio then?"

"Sure." Gus is calmer than I am, but that isn't unlike them.

We say goodbye and Georgie squeals. "This might be happening!"

We get a few looks from nearby stage techs but thankfully this isn't abnormal behavior for us, so no one thinks twice. I fly through the rest of rehearsal in a daze. I wonder what changed with Gus, and I hope they didn't get broken up with or anything because of the photo. Gus said it wasn't serious but I don't fully understand what that means. Hopefully they'll be able to explain it tonight. I take the quickest shower in my dressing room and change into something comfortable. It's easier to hide from the media when I'm dressed casually and my tattoos are covered. My driver takes me to the studio, and this time, I let them walk me in just in case there's a crowd again. Since there isn't, I text Gus, but the second I do, they unlock the door for me.

"Sorry, we had to close early today because we had too many people stopping by in hopes of seeing you. We're only taking appointments in the meantime," Gus explains as they walk me toward their room. I pass River working on a client and she smiles.

"No worries, I can always send over some security if you guys need it. I don't want you to be inconvenienced because of me."

"We appreciate that." Gus smiles.

They lead me into an office instead of the room they tattooed me in. They sit behind the desk and gesture for me to take a seat across from them.

"I thought we'd have more privacy in here. River said it's soundproof for meetings. We think a law firm used to be in this space," Gus explains.

"Ah. Thank you for that." I nod.

"So, I want you to give me as much detail about what you're looking for as you can."

"Can I ask something first?" They nod, so I continue. "Did something happen with the person you were seeing? I only ask since that seemed to be the reason you were against the idea."

Gus sighs. "So I guess if this is going to work, we'll have to be transparent with each other. Basically, I really like this woman. And I'd love nothing more than to be with her exclusively and committed, but she's hesitant because of her past, so we've been taking things slow. She's seeing someone else and we're open for now. She's very hot and cold but for the first time in months, she's been more hot because of our photo together. She got kind of jealous. So since it's not real anyway, I was thinking that I could make her jealous by publicly dating you, putting off her advances until our timeline is up."

"Wow. I was not expecting that," I admit. "You know this will have to be a commitment of at least six months minimum?"

"I do. And that's okay with me. I'm willing to play the long game if it means getting to be with her."

"Okay. Then yeah, I would need you to come to my concerts, hang out backstage. There are certain obligations and events my manager would request your attendance at. And in between that, we'd need to go on several public outings to prove we're a real couple. We don't want anyone knowing the truth, obviously," I explain.

"And who would know the truth?"

"Georgie, my manager, and if you have a best friend or someone you feel like you need to tell. The less who know about it, the better."

"I don't need to tell anyone," Gus says.

"We obviously would need to keep it professional and not actually fall for each other. This isn't some kind of rom com," I joke.

"You don't have to worry about me," Gus says with a chuckle.

"You'll have to be okay with being in the limelight, and depending on how things go, we might need to get a bodyguard —" Gus starts to make a face, "At least at your house and at the shop here. Fans can be a little nuts."

"Fine." They grimace.

"What about what you'd like to be called? I know you go by they/them, so how would you prefer I refer to you?"

"I wish there was a cooler word than partner, it sounds like we're gay cowboys. But partner works. I appreciate you being aware and asking me that."

"I don't want to assume. I'll make it clear in posts and when speaking about you. I can't guarantee the press won't have shit to say because sadly that's the kind of world we live in." I sigh.

"What about like…kissing? Or public displays of affection?" Gus blushes as they ask.

"We can discuss specifics; it would obviously be like acting. I'm comfortable with holding hands, kissing, being touched—

like if you touch my face or hold my waist. But if there's anything you're not comfortable with, I will be sure to make note."

"I-I uh, think I'm fine with everything," Gus says.

"Viv, my manager, gave me a contract I have to have you sign. It's basically an NDA saying you won't tell anyone about us being fake or about anything that could hurt me or my career. It's pretty standard but if you need a lawyer to look at it, I understand." I hand it to them, and they start to look it over.

They take their time reading each page before they sign and initial wherever they need to. They hand it back to me and smile.

"So, what now?"

"Well, the media will see me leaving here again. Maybe you could walk me down? Another hug wouldn't be the worst thing, and this time we'd be expecting it. I'm going on a podcast tomorrow morning, and I'm sure it'll be one of the first things I'm asked about. Once that's out in the open, then we'll plan our first public outing and compare schedules."

"Got it, that all sounds good." Gus nods.

"Oh, and feel free to bring that girl you're trying to impress to my concert. It might ruffle her feathers that you'd bring her to see me. It would definitely make me jealous." I smirk.

"You wouldn't mind?" Gus looks surprised.

"You're doing me a huge favor. I'm sure the money has a little to do with it, but trust me, helping you out in the relation-ship department too is the least I can do."

"Oh, I don't want the money." Gus frowns.

"What?"

"I didn't see it mentioned on the contract, so I didn't think to say anything. I'm not looking for financial compensation. I'm set and we're both helping each other, it wouldn't feel right to me." Gus shrugs.

"Well, if you change your mind, the offer stands."

I stand, feeling more relaxed than when I walked through the front door. Gus walks me out toward the elevator and as soon as

I step outside, I spot the paparazzi. They aren't doing a very good job at hiding, but I guess that's how they get the better shots.

Gus pulls me in for a hug, and this time it feels different. Their body presses against mine and in a shock, I forget how to breathe. I can feel my pulse racing, and I almost forget to smile for the cameras. Their hands stay on the top of my waist, holding me steady as I wrap my arms around their neck. They've got a few inches on me but right now, all I can feel is their warmth and the smell of cherries. Is it their Chapstick? Some sort of hand sanitizer? I can't put my finger on it, but soon we were pulling apart.

"I'll see you soon, babe." Gus adds a wink for good measure.

Without thinking about it, or forcing it, I'm blushing and smiling goodbye. In a daze, I walk to the car and get in. What the hell was wrong with me? It's like Gus put some kind of a magical spell on me. I know better than that, but somehow, I forgot how good it felt just to be held by someone. But the thought of Gus's wink and their extra-long hug lingers in a way that makes my body buzz.

I needed to get home and use my vibrator. I can't be out in life right now while I feel like this. Trying to do the math in my head, I can't remember the last time I got laid. If I were smart, I would've hooked up with someone before I got into a six-month long commitment with someone. But here I am doing without thinking. I'll have to make sure my vibrator is charged at all times for the upcoming months. Or I'll be radiating this energy every time my fake partner touches me.

By the time the driver drops me off at home, I'm racing to the bedroom to take care of this. The last thing I need is to be so stupidly horny that I make a move on my fake partner and ruin the whole thing. Our first and most important rule is that we can't go falling for each other. Surely, that will happen or at least become complicated if we hook up.

EIGHT

Gus

For the second time in my life, I made headlines for hugging a woman. It's not as huge as it seems, but you'd think I learned how to cure cancer or something. The fact that I called her babe even made it into most of the news outlets. I was being named the 'unnamed, hot and sweet tattoo artist girlfriend' of LULY. I didn't love the girlfriend part of it, but it was understandable. Emily was an out and proud lesbian, so of course she was to be assumed to be dating a woman. As long as Emily knew how I liked to be referred to, I was fine with it.

Today was supposed to be our first public outing as a couple, and I was nervous as fuck. She had gone on the podcast and said I was her partner. She had put everything into motion for our plan, and it was going fine so far. It was working well for me too; I had Cari asking to see me. She wouldn't come right out and ask me about Emily, but I knew she was dying for details. I kept her out of the loop, being coy with my replies and saying I was busy. I had a chat with her about how I'm seeing how things go with someone, and I think they're getting serious. She was completely shocked, and I can tell she was jealous too, but she tried not to make that part so obvious. She said she understood, and she would be around if things didn't work out. But in the meantime, she made it clear she wanted to stay friends. Of course, she winked when she said that part, so I don't know exactly what it means. But she's been more on than off so I'm not complaining.

Emily asked to meet me in Brooklyn—she said she never gets the chance to go because of work. But she managed to convince her manager it was important for her image. I'm standing next to this cute little bakery right off Dumbo. It's a little touristy, but it isn't bad for the middle of the day. I'm looking around for her when I spot two tufts of blonde hair and a blur of pink. Sure enough, Emily is walking down the street. She has two body-guards behind her in all black and sunglasses. Her hair is in these bun-looking things on the top of her head with two curls in the front of her face. She's wearing a pink crop top that she has tied up to expose the edges of the bottom of her new tattoo. Her legs are mostly covered by a black floral skirt except for a sliver of her leg when she walks. I told her to wear comfortable shoes, so I was relieved to see her in a pair of flat black boots.

"Hey!" Emily waves big and smiles as she sees me.

"Hey, babe." It feels weird but I guess it's something I'd have to get used to it.

"These are my bodyguards, Bill and Rob. They will be following us but not close. The label insisted they come along," Emily explains.

"Boys." I nod. They keep stoic expressions like those guards at Buckingham palace.

"I'm so excited. I never get the full day off." Emily smiles.

"Happy to show you around. I've lived in Brooklyn for more than a decade."

"Wow, you're like a transplant New Yorker, then? Where did you move from?" Emily asks.

"This tiny town in New Jersey, I prefer not to think about," I joke. "I've lived in New York almost longer than I did that town."

"Got it. I was born in a small town too, in Seaside, Oregon. No one ever talks about it. They mention Portland and I'm like yeah, like an hour from there." She laughs.

We start walking and sure enough the guards keep a distance. I lead her toward the waterfront; I had set up a picnic over there with a perfect view of the Brooklyn Bridge.

"Then you get it." I laugh.

"Oh my gosh! Is someone having a picnic? This is too cute!" She gasps as we walk up the steps and see the picnic I've set up.

"We are." I smile proudly; I was a little nervous of my idea but now I'm feeling relieved.

"We are?!" Emily gasps and I nod.

She walks over to the light blue sheet and takes everything in. I have a literal picnic basket, an array of snacks, and a bottle of champagne. Emily takes a seat, and I sit down across from her.

"Wow, this view is amazing." Emily looks ahead of her. The water is extra blue since it's early in the season. It looks extra clean today. The Brooklyn Bridge is bustling, as usual, and the water crashes into the rocks at the shore nearby.

"I like coming here to draw sometimes," I say.

"This is so cool, you didn't have to do all of this."

"We're dating, just because it's not...*you know*, doesn't mean I wouldn't pull out all the stops like you're my girl." I wink.

"Well, consider me impressed." Emily smiles. She glances behind me and then looks back at me. I'm about to ask when she mouths the word '*paparazzi*'. Wow, that didn't take long at all.

"So, tell me more about you. What can I learn that isn't in the media?" I ask.

"Hmm, well, I always wanted to be a fashion designer. When I was a kid, I had a sketch book full of ideas and I thought about going for it, but I'm a terrible artist and a good singer, so I chose this route instead." She shrugs. I pull out some of the food from the basket and take note of what she chooses to eat. Emily takes the cheese and nuts but leaves the crackers alone.

"I bet you're not that bad."

"I literally had to sketch something for my best friend recently, to explain where we'd put our new painting, and she was so confused. She thought I was trying to play charades with her."

"Oof. So you live with Georgie then?"

"Yup, we lived together since we moved out here. It took a little more convincing to Georgie, but she got into law school, and I was moving here anyway."

"So she's a lawyer then?"

"No, actually she took one semester of law school and hated it. So she works on Wall Street now, I don't know her official title but she enjoys it."

"As long as it's something she enjoys." I smile.

"How'd you get into tattooing?"

"I stumbled into it. I didn't want to go to college, so I decided to apply for a tattoo apprenticeship on a whim. It was a lot of work, and my teacher was an asshat, but after that I went to a shop with a woman who taught me everything I know. She was a butch and ran a shop that made me feel safe. I stayed with her until I met River, Isla, and Rae and we formed RARE's," I explain.

"That makes sense. You're incredibly talented, I'm glad you figured out what you like to do so easily."

I pause. "Do you not like the crackers I brought?"

"Oh, no it's just that I'm gluten free," Emily says shyly.

"Shit, like, they can't even touch the gluten? I didn't know, I'm so sorry."

"No, no it's okay. I have PCOS, and I've found that going gluten free helps my symptoms just a bit. So I'm not allergic or anything, but I don't eat gluten. Except for super rare occasions," she explains.

"Got it, definitely good to know for our next date."

"Next date? You're already planning a second one?" She smirks.

"Well, yes? I like planning them," I admit.

"Sounds perfect to me, I'm very good at being told when and where to show up."

I pour her a glass of the champagne into a plastic cup, and she holds it out to me.

"It's bad luck not to toast a bottle of champagne," she says.

"Ah, then what do we toast to?"

She pauses, thinking about it for a moment. "To new beginnings."

"To new beginnings," I agree.

We finish up the snacks and pack away the picnic for now. I tuck it into a secret hiding spot behind one of the bushes, so we don't have to carry it. If someone took it, it wouldn't be the end of the world, but I've done this before. I figure it's safe.

"Shall we?" I hold out my hand and Emily takes it happily.

Her small hand slips into mine and I smile. It fits like a glove. While my hands are pretty bare except for my watch, hers are covered in array of gold rings and a few bracelets. Our hands intertwine naturally, and I lead the way toward Brooklyn Bridge Park.

"Is that a carousel? Can we go?" she asks excitedly.

"Sure, why not?"

We grab two tickets for the carousel and there's only two other families getting on the ride. What is the funniest is me catching one of the bodyguards—I can't remember which one—riding on it as well. I guess they needed to be close to Emily in an emergency, but it looked hysterical seeing this huge football player-type standing next to a painted horse statue. We take a seat on the bench, and Emily looks happier than the children who are screaming to get off. We're probably going three miles per hour, but she looks relaxed as we look over the water.

"I can never look at carousels the same…"

I cut her off. "After Cassie's scene in *Euphoria*?!"

"Yes!" We're both hysterical laughing at the thought of that scene. I don't know how it was supposed to be hot; it was crazy to me. Why would getting off on a carousel in front of hundreds of strangers be hot?

"Could you imagine? I doubt it's possible, it doesn't go fast enough," Emily muses.

"Maybe when you're on the drugs she was on," I say.

"That's true." We both laugh just thinking about it.

Emily's hand finds mine again as we walk through the park. We talk about things that we like and dislike. We're not sure if the paparazzi are following us, so we don't talk about anything we don't want overheard. Truthfully, it's a nice opportunity to get to know her. I didn't know much about her, and it made sense that we should at least try to get to know the other. It would only take one question about her favorite food or color that could blow this whole thing up. Not that I was going to be doing any talking to the press.

We stop along the water to look at the passing boats and the kids playing in the park. There are grassy areas where people are tanning and reading. We're both pretty quiet when a breeze blows by and the loose curls Emily has get caught in her lip gloss. Before she does anything, I reach forward to help tuck the loose strands behind her ears. She looks up at me, and her blue eyes melt into mine for just a moment. Everything nearby is suddenly silent, and I wonder if she's about to kiss me. We both talked about it, it was something we were comfortable with. But I never anticipated it to feel so intimate. Her hand catches mine and my breathing stills. I think about leaning in to close the distance, but I don't want to read the situation wrong. I don't know if I'm reading into things or not.

At the last moment, Emily leans in, and just as I close my eyes, thinking she's about to kiss me, she instead whispers in my ear. "There's a paparazzi right behind you, so make this look good."

Of course, this was all in my head. I knew what I signed up for, yet I was falling for an impressively good actress. I press my lips to the top of her head, breathing in a sweet minty smell. Maybe eucalyptus? It's relaxing, but she pulls away and we continue our date.

NINE

Emily

I'm relieved at how easy it is to pretend to be with Gus. It feels like I'm just hanging out with a good friend. They hold my hand and call me babe, and I've never laughed that hard on a date with someone. It's a relief, and I forgot we were supposed to be putting on a show for the cameras. But even without thinking about it, we manage to get amazing photos because of how natural we are. Viv made a point of telling me how good this is on the way to the Sesame Street shoot. We're filming in the Kaufman Astoria studios, which is in Queens, so at least I don't have to get on a plane for this.

Currently, I'm in hair and makeup with Viv sitting next to me on her phone. She's typing away, working on something, and I sigh. I'm not thrilled to be doing this, but I know it will help. Viv hasn't steered me wrong yet, so I take her advice. I mean, that's what I pay her for. The makeup artist finishes, and I'm swept into wardrobe. I offered to bring clothes, but I think they wanted to make sure I'm wearing something appropriate. They give me a pink, oversized T-shirt and a pink flannel that matches, along with a pair of ripped jeans with patches sewn under. I'm allowed to keep my boots on, and I'm led to set.

My team takes photos of me with the whole gang; I even

manage to get some selfies with Elmo. They had me prepping the song all week, so I'm not worried. It's a cute kids' song about feelings made up to the tune of one of my songs. So I know how to sing it. There is a teleprompter in case I need it, but I'm not worried. I've had enough practice, and I could sing it in my sleep at this point. The only thing that's weird is I have to sing with the puppets and not give any attention or indication to the puppeteers actually doing the work. It's essentially like singing and dancing with a figment of my imagination. No wonder they said Steve from Blue's Clues went nuts.

"Okay sweetie. We say action, you count to three and then start singing. The puppets will join in after you, and it's important that you don't move when you're. Just stay on set and talk to Elmo or Cookie or whoever you like," the director tells me. I don't appreciate him calling me sweetie, but he's old and this is Sesame Street, so I'm going to let it slide.

"Sounds good." I force a smile.

Viv is in the background, reminding me to smile, so I do. I need this over as soon as possible, so I'm not in the mood to do fifty takes.

"Action!" One. Two. Three.

I start singing the lyrics I memorized, the puppets start dancing not too long after. As I keep going, I dance a little, getting into it. Viv and the director look pleased as I sing the song and dance with Elmo. It doesn't feel as crazy if I don't think about it too much. As soon as the song is done, the music continues, and I blow the camera a kiss before doing a little shimmy with Big Bird.

"Cut!" the director calls. "I think that's the first time we've gotten it on the first take."

"Should we do it again, just in case?" one of the production assistants asks the director nervously.

"Yes. Always do it again just in case. Things happen all the time and it's better to have a backup." He nods.

"You need a drink or anything, Emily?" the director asks.

"No thank you, I'm good to go." I smile.

We do the number once more, just in case, and everyone seems happy. Security escorts Viv and me back to the car and we head back into the city. I text Gus a photo of me with Elmo. I don't know why I do, but we've been texting a lot lately.

GUS: Excuse me, you didn't take a photo with *the* Cookie Monster?!

ME: I did! But I don't have it on my phone. You'll have to watch the episode

GUS: Already have a note in my phone. I think I turned on your post notifications on IG too

ME: Sounds like someone is becoming quite a stalker

GUS: Only because I have such a beautiful girlfriend 😊

I'm the one blushing now. Gus flirts with me often, but it's all part of the plan. Viv looks over my shoulder and smiles after reading the texts.

"That's cute. You should post that." She says over her glasses.

"Our texts?" I look at her, confused.

"Yes, it shows it's not all for show. Good job on making this look real."

"We—" I stop myself; it isn't worth it to explain to her this *is* real. "I'm not posting our texts." Gus wouldn't want that. *I* don't want that. There has to be some things that belong to just us.

"Okay, but I want a photo of you two posted soon."

"I posted them on my story last week." I sigh.

"You have to make it grid official," she says like it's obvious.

"Okay." I nod.

I'm not seeing Gus again until Thursday, but I guess we'll be taking some photos together. It has to match my grid, so it has to be something artsy. I rarely post on my grid; it's too much pressure. The comments, the influx of DMs, people telling me it looks bad or begging for the new album. I wish there was a way just to get notifications from the people I actually follow. Sure, I have a secret account like everyone does, but it isn't the same.

I glance at Gus's account; it's mostly tattoos they've done with the occasional selfie. The last one was the day of River and Aspen's wedding. Gus was in a tux and their hair was slicked back, sleeves rolled up to show off their tattoo sleeves. They looked hot as fuck, if I'm being honest.

"Your show on Saturday is going to have extra press and media after the show. I want Gus to be there with you for it. They can sit in the VIP section and then join you in the green room after the show. Okay?"

"I mean, I have to check with their schedule but that's fine with me."

"Their schedule?" Viv scoffs.

"Yes, they run a very successful business. I have to make sure they can take the time away."

"Fine, but they need to be there. Hopefully she can make a night away from her *successful business*," Viv mocks.

"They." I correct.

"What?" She looks at me, confused.

"Gus uses they/them pronouns. I told you this, but you just called them 'she'. Make sure it doesn't happen in front of them," I say firmly.

"Fine." Viv rolls her eyes. But she knows I mean business because I don't typically give her such a hard time about things.

We're quiet for the rest of the ride, aside from Viv's typing with her long nails until we arrive at the theater we booked for rehearsal. It's only a few blocks from the concert venue and has a similar size in stage. The band is already there getting ready, and I need to get changed into my workout clothes. I work up a sweat while I'm practicing for a show. I want to give it my all, and the more I practice the moves during the rehearsals, the easier the performances are.

Georgie is at work today, so I'm alone in practice. I know

some of the dancers, but not very well. Viv and the team are always switching them out whenever they felt like it, so I don't get attached to them. It isn't something I have much control over like the band. So I kept my opinions about that to myself.

"Have you had time to learn the new choreo?" my production manager asks me.

"Only the first two songs. But we can run through everything, so I know what I need more help with," I tell her. She nods.

"Okay everyone, we're doing a full run through, from start to finish, and I don't want anyone passing out, so please take your water breaks," she commands. I don't remember her name; she's new-ish. My old choreographer/production manager went on maternity leave a few weeks ago. She has the cutest little girl named Natalie, and I sent a gift basket of baby clothes. I don't think I ever personally want kids, but I do love how cute they were.

I start in the front, running through the first two songs with no issues. The third song is fine, but it's the fourth one that I'm having trouble with. It's the faster songs that I'm not used to yet. The choreographer takes the time to go over everything with me again, and I focus so I don't miss anything. I'm a pretty good dancer, but it isn't something that comes naturally to me, like singing. I need to practice to nail the moves, which isn't normally an issue, but I have a little more pressure than normal.

Viv is in my ear (not literally), reminding me that media reps are coming this weekend. They will be watching my every move and waiting to report on my mistakes. Not to mention, it'll be the first time Gus sees me play live. I know they saw me last year playing Aspen's birthday, but that was nothing compared to this stage. What if they see me live and how much pop music I play, and they hate it? What if they see how much I have to compromise to be on the big stage, and they don't understand it?

Some days, I hate how much I've had to give up for the sake of being on stage. But I know, in the long run, it's something I'll appreciate. When I prove to the label that I know what I'm doing and I can be successful, they'll give me the chance to do what I want. They let me record some of my emotional songs for the first album. They're already pushing for me to write more stuff for the second album. It would be crazy of them to keep me consistently making pop music for the rest of my life. They wanted me to grow with my music, and that is exactly what I want.

They call a water break, and I chug down a few sips of my electrolyte water. The last thing I need is my sugar going too low and being the one to pass out. I tie up my hair with my pink scrunchie and take a deep breath. We keep running through the songs and the moves. For some reason, Viv is nowhere in sight. She's normally on the side of the stage, taking notes on me. It's a bit of a relief not to see that, but part of me is worried. Is something bigger going on that she had to deal with? I shake it off and focus on my dancing.

"Good! Just like that, Lu!" the choreographer says.

I go by Lu or LULY to everyone who doesn't know my real name. It isn't like it's a huge secret, but I like going by a stage name. It keeps the illusion that I can leave things on the stage. Like, there isn't an immense amount of pressure to be *Emily*. She's a *normal* person; she didn't have to worry about the kinds of things LULY does. I finally understand how Hannah Montana felt.

TEN

Gus

"So are you going to give us the tea about your new girlfriend? Or do we have to read about it on Page Six?" Isla teases as we gather around for the monthly team meeting.

"I don't know what you're talking about," I lie.

"Are you kidding?! You are so secretive! You don't mention that you're dating an iconic lesbian pop star?" Isla exclaims.

I laugh. "I mean, you know that part."

"I think Isla is talking about the fact that you got caught hugging her and now you're all official?" Rae adds. I wish River were here, she'd get us off this topic.

"Sorry I'm late, Aspen brought us lunch since it's Thursday, but I forgot to tell her it's the monthly meeting. She forgot to read the calendar again." River shakes her head as she plops a bag of fast food on the meeting room table. "Oh, and she brought your protein shake." River hands me the peanut butter banana protein shake she brings me every Thursday. The place right by their apartment has the best protein shakes. It tastes more like a milkshake.

"Good, you're just in time. We're talking about Gus's girl-friend," Isla says.

"No, we aren't." I shake my head.

"I'm curious about that myself, but I'm not going to pry," River admits.

"There's nothing to tell. We hit it off and we kept things quiet until we were sure it would work out." I shrug.

"Makes sense," Rae says. Isla goes to open her mouth, but Rae stops her.

"Anyway, as usual, I'll go over the sales for the month, chat about any pending issues or growth, and then we can discuss individually if there's anything you need. Feel free to eat but silence all phones," River says, turning into corporate mode.

River goes into specifics about the number of clients we had, the number of sales we had, and how we did better this month than last month. We've been on a steady uphill climb as we grow the business. We're coming up on the three-year anniversary of the shop opening and have discussed throwing some kind of event, but everything is still a work in progress. There are no unpaid bills this month, and we had a larger profit than normal. We're close to paying the mortgage off on this space, and River proposes the idea of hiring more staff.

"So, with the influx of clientele from all of us, but especially Gus's new girlfriend, it might be time to hire a front desk assistant and another artist or two. Thoughts?" River says.

"I don't want to post publicly about the openings; I'm afraid we'll just get fans trying to get a peek of LULY and not anyone actually interested in the job," I say.

"I agree, which is why I'd like to reach out to several companies who do the vetting for us. They post the openings, reach out to their clients, and then let us know whose interested and qualified," River explains.

"That sounds good," Rae says, and we all nod.

"We have the budget to hire two new tattoo artists and one receptionist at the present time. I would like them all to be full time, and they'd have their own office and the chance to build their own client list, just like we did," River explains. "Now that's about it for me, does anyone have more to add?"

"Yes, I was thinking about the anniversary event. What if we throw a party? We could do flash tattoos and invite apprentices and other artists to do tattoos. Maybe like a gala sort of event where buying a tattoo is a donation to the studio?" Isla offers.

"I really like that idea," I admit.

"So many other studios do small things, but what if we went big? The bigger tattoo lovers would love the chance to get an exclusive tattoo. Maybe only one of each design? To make it exclusive," Isla goes on.

"Wow, it seems like you've given this a lot of thought," River says.

"I have; it's something I'd love to run point on, if that's okay with you." Isla smiles.

"All in favor?" River asks. She runs the meetings and takes care of a lot of the paperwork, but everything around here is discussed and voted on. No one of us has more power than the other. We all put the same amount into this business, and we run it as such.

We all vote in favor of Isla running the event. It seems well thought out, and I know she's not going to run off with our money or spend it on anything that won't be beneficial to us.

"Thanks guys, I won't let you down." She smiles.

"Gus, due to your influx in media popularity, this decision will be completely up to you. But I was thinking, maybe for the time being, you'll only be taking on appointments. For the most part, the bookings have subsided back to normal. But there's still an influx of requests for you, and rather than disappoint every-one, I was thinking you could check the request forms and choose the ones you want to do, then let the rest know another artist is available if you can't. Would that work for you?" River asks.

"Yeah, I obviously don't want to take clients from anyone,

but I do appreciate it. It might be nice to have a little more of a set schedule than waiting for walk-ins too," I admit.

"Not an issue. I think you should request a 50% deposit for everyone booking online, just to weed out the ones just hoping to get a photo with you or LULY," River adds.

"Good point." I nod. Our normal policy was a nonrefundable $50 deposit, but 50% will probably be more than that.

"That's about it for today, unless anyone has something to add."

"Actually, I do." I raise my hand. "Emily invited all of us to her concert on Saturday night. I have VIP passes for everyone and extras for any plus ones." I pull the tickets out of my folder on the table and hand out two to each of them.

"Holy shit, this is like front row, basically." Rae gasps.

"It's more like a VIP box. I think I'll be backstage, but she wanted to make sure everyone got one. I also have one for Cari if you don't mind getting it to her." I hand the extra ticket to River.

"Holy shit, she's going to be so excited." River smiles.

"Thank you, Gus." Isla smiles.

"No worries. Emily wants the chance to meet my friends and thought this would be a fun way to get together."

"Hell yes. I'll be there." River nods. I knew it wouldn't be hard to convince her to see her favorite singer. "Aspen is going to go insane; you just got me the ticket to the best sex ever."

"Eww. I do not need to know that." I grimace. River is like a little sister to me. I do not need to think of her like that. Isla, Rae, and River all start laughing.

We head out of the meeting and Aspen is waiting for River in the lobby. She greets me with a smile. "Thanks for the shake, it's so good."

"Of course, don't forget about me when you become famous," Aspen teases.

"I'm not becoming famous; it's my girlfriend who's famous." I shrug. The word slips off my tongue easier than I anticipated.

"I didn't know it was so serious." Aspen winks.

"I guess when you know, you know." I wish I wasn't having this conversation.

Cari and I are still texting, and although we haven't seen each other since I started dating Emily, it isn't like the door is shut. She's been texting me even more, and I don't know what it means or how she feels. It was Emily's idea for me to give an extra ticket to Cari. I think she thought it would help make her jealous, and she's probably right. It's hard not to look at Emily and be jealous; she's beautiful and talented.

"Don't bother, babe. They said they aren't giving out any details of their relationship," River says, placing a kiss on Aspen's cheek.

"How's your ankle? You look good," I say to change the subject.

"It was a little sprain. I *might* have overreacted at the time, but I didn't know. It hurt like a bitch." Aspen turns red with embarrassment.

"But it all worked out, because that was the night Gus did LULY's tattoo." River adds.

"Ah, that's true."

So much for getting the subject off me and Emily. I don't want to lie to my friends if I don't have to. It's one thing to make it more than it is for the press but telling my friends stuff that isn't true isn't going to help anyone.

"I actually have to get going, I have a few things to do tonight," I say looking at my watch.

"You mean, someone to do?" Isla teases.

"No, I mean doing my laundry, you horny bastards." I shake my head with a small smile.

I grab my things and head downstairs. There isn't anyone hanging around tonight, so I head to the subway without any issues. I need to do my laundry, pick up some cat food, and maybe hit the gym. I'm meeting Emily tomorrow for our second official date after work. We're going out to dinner, so it's going to be pretty casual, but I don't want to show up in dirty work clothes. Plus, with the concert this weekend, I want to make sure I have something nice to wear to that too.

EMILY: did you give ur friends da tix?
    ME: yes! All should be there 😌
    EMILY: yay! Can't wait to meet them!
    ME: sorry in advance if they fangirl over you
    EMILY: I'd be offended if they didn't
    ME: 😂😄
    EMILY: are we still good for tomorrow?
    ME: yup. What time?
    EMILY: what time r u done with work?
    ME: uh 7? 7:30?
    EMILY: let's do dinner @ 8
    EMILY: I'll pick u up
    ME: I don't mind meeting you there
    EMILY: no! It's a date! I'm picking you up
    ME: as long as I don't have to wear a dress
    EMILY: damn, I thought we'd wear matching sparkly ones
    ME: you are on your own there, babe
    EMILY: are you flirting with me? 😈
    ME: of course 😊

Emily and I make a point not to talk about the fact that this is fake over text. We know how easily our phones or social media can be hacked. The last thing we need is a scandal because we sent a text to the wrong person. But sometimes I forget I don't *need* to flirt with her, it just sort of comes out naturally. Like this sort of banter we did back and forth. I call her babe, I send those flirty emojis, and I call her mine. It just seems normal, and it isn't something she's ever brought up when we were together, so I guess it's fine. It's not like there are rules on how to be someone's fake partner. And it isn't exactly something I can google. Can people hack what famous people google? It seems likely.

I'm not nervous about dinner tomorrow night; I was actually looking forward to it. I don't know where we are going, but I figure it's easier to let Emily pick. She has dietary restrictions, and she knows if and where media might be. I'm in it for the free food and the company. She insists on paying for dinner, even though it goes against everything I stand for. But she claims it comes out of the company's budget, not hers, so that makes me feel a little bit better.

ELEVEN

Emily

The driver is outside my place before I'm ready, so I ask Georgie to tell them I need five minutes. I'm putting on my mascara and the finishing touches on my lips, plus I still need to put my shoes on.

"Damn, you look hot," Georgie says.

"Thanks. We're going to this fancy steak place uptown, so I want to look nice," I explain.

"Gus won't be able to keep their hands off you, for real."

"Nah, they don't think of me that way."

"Psssh, okay." She chuckles.

"What?" I turn around and raise an eyebrow.

"Every time you're photographed together, Gus looks at you like they like you. I know you said this is all fake, but I wouldn't be surprised if they're starting to fall for you." Georgie shrugs.

"I—I do not have time to argue this with you but trust me, it's all for show."

Georgie puts her hand to her mouth and makes the 'zipping her lips' motion.

Rolling my eyes, I grab my heels and head for the elevator. I quickly put them on while it brings me to the parking garage under the building. My driver and bodyguard are in the front seat, and they open the door for me. I send a quick text to let Gus know I'm on the way and they say okay.

I put my phone down on the seat next to me and smooth out my dress. Which is sort of pointless because it's that satin type of fabric that looks better when it has some wrinkles to it. I don't know why I'm suddenly nervous, but it's probably because of what Georgie said to me before I left. I know Gus and I have been flirting more lately in person and over text, but it's all for show. We're making it look realistic. It's not like they're falling for me; they knew what this is. I'm sure Georgie is just reading into things.

We pull up and Gus isn't outside, so I get out of the car, click clack my heels into the building, and almost slam into them coming out of the elevator.

"I'm sorry!" I say first.

"I didn't realize you were coming in, I'm sorry." Gus smiles. They look me over, my face first, stopping at my chest briefly, and all the way down my body, and then they frown.

"What?" Did my dress have a rip in it or something?

"I'm underdressed." Gus frowns. They're in a black T-shirt and a pair of black jeans.

"Oh, this is what you're wearing?" I sort of thought they were still in work clothes.

"Yeah…is the place fancy? I didn't realize." They sigh.

"It is…" Now I feel shitty; I should've told Gus where we were going and how fancy it was going to be. I was just focused on getting gluten-free food and making sure I looked okay.

"I'm sorry—"

"Nonsense, let's just go somewhere else," I decide.

"Are you sure? I thought this place was…chosen carefully?" They raise an eyebrow.

"It was, but realistically, it takes five seconds for someone to spot me and paparazzi to follow me."

"Do you have another place in mind?"

"No, but we can walk around and find something? There has to be something gluten-free around here," I say.

"Now I feel bad—"

I cut Gus off again. "It's my bad. I should've told you how to dress; that's totally on me. As long as we find food, I'm happy to go anywhere." I smile.

"Okay, I think I know a place. If you trust me."

"Oh God, should I be scared?" I pause.

"Nah, I think you'll like it." Gus holds out their hand and I take it eagerly.

They lead me out the front door and we stop to tell the driver what's going on. My bodyguard doesn't like the idea, but I felt safe with Gus. I somehow know they wouldn't let anything happen to me. So we walk down the street, pausing for the lights to change, and slip into the crowd. That is one of the great things about New York—I can pass for a nobody. Even all dressed up, no one gives a shit because everyone is in their own head about their own stuff. New Yorkers are selfish in the best way.

"Will you tell me where we're going?" I ask.

"Nope. But trust me, there's no dress code." They chuckle.

I follow them through the bustling streets, holding onto their hand tightly. They make sure people make space for me and I'm safe. I keep my head down for the most part, hoping I can keep some anonymity for now. We stop walking and end up on Fifty-eighth Street, right in front of this bright red taco truck. I can't see the name from where I'm standing, but the menu is short—only six items—and there are pictures of each one on the side.

"Is this where we're eating?" I ask.

"Yes, they use corn tortillas so that's okay, right?" Gus checks.

"Yeah." I smile. "I love tacos." Of course, I can't remember the last time I actually ate a taco in the last year, but I do love them.

"Order whatever you want and it's on *me*," Gus says, seeing if I'll argue with them about paying. It's kind of misogynistic of them to insist on paying for me, but I decide to let this one slide. I guess I like being taken care of.

"Fine, I guess I'll let my partner pay for me." I fake an eye roll and Gus laughs.

"Hey! Gus!" The man in the truck recognizes Gus and gives them a big smile. "Your usual?"

"Yes please, and whatever she wants. It's date night." Gus winks and the guy smiles.

"You're very lucky; Gus never brings anyone to my truck. You must be someone special," the man says.

Before I can speak, Gus adds, "She is." My gaze darts to them and Gus smiles at me longingly. My stomach turns to butterflies, and I have to shake the feeling away. What the hell is happening?

"I'll have three chicken tacos and a side of Guacamole and sour cream, please," I say.

"Coming right up," the man says, and Gus hands them a twenty, then places a five in the tip jar—which is really just an old container with a hole cut in the top.

"You really never bring anyone here? I thought you had a thing with someone?" I ask quietly as we step to the side to wait for our food.

"I did, but I don't bring just anyone here. It's my favorite food truck in the city." Gus shrugs.

I don't know why that has such an effect on me. But before I have a chance to overthink about it, the food is ready. We're handed an open container with tacos that smell divine. I outwardly groan.

"Yeah, and they taste just as good." Gus smirks.

"Where are we eating these? Is there somewhere to sit?" I look around but I don't see anywhere.

"Nope, we eat them right here. If you try to find somewhere they get cold."

"I can't exactly eat tacos one handed on the side of the street," I say.

"Yes, you can, try it," Gus insists and waits for me to try.

I let out a deep breath and hold the plate with one hand and lift a taco with the other. It's hot and some of it drips out onto the plate, so I hold it tighter. Pulling it to my mouth, I smell the mix of cilantro, salsa, avocados, grilled chicken, and sour cream mixing together. I take a larger bite than I normally would, and the food melts in my mouth. Holy shit, Gus is right. This might be the best taco I've ever had. *insert lesbian joke here* But seriously, it's that good.

"So?" Gus prompts.

"It's amazing." I nod.

Gus smiles and digs into theirs. I watch as they hold it over the plate so if any food falls out, it lands on the other tacos. I do the same, holding it a few inches from my body to make sure it doesn't fall on my dress either. I'm eating the last taco when I get sour cream all over my face. I can't help but laugh as Gus notices and tries not to laugh, holding out a napkin, but I have no hands to take it. They wipe the sour cream off my face and we're both in hysterics.

"Thank you, I'm not so sure a photo of me with white stuff all over my face would go over well with my manager," I joke.

"Definitely would make people confused about us." Gus laughs.

We finish our tacos and grab two bottles of water. I'm drinking mine when I catch Gus looking at my chest. I'm about to say something when they catch my gaze.

"I realize it looks like I'm checking out your chest, but in reality, I'm trying to make sure your tattoo is healing okay." Gus blushes.

"I bet that's what you tell all the girls," I tease.

"I swear! I only ever see tattoos months later, if that. I just wanted to make sure there are no issues," Gus explains.

I decide to tease them, pulling my dress down slightly so they can see a little more of my tattoo. I'm not wearing a bra, so they can probably see even more than I realize. "How's it look?" I ask innocently.

Gus gulps, their eyes looking anywhere but at me while their cheeks turn a bright red. "Looks good." Their voice cracks and I lose it.

"Anyway, would you like to go somewhere else now?" I ask.

"Sure, what did you have in mind?"

"We can just walk until we see something to do." I shrug.

"Is that, like, safe?" Gus looks around and then back at me.

"It's fine," I assure them. Honestly, it could go either way, but I'm not someone who likes to live in fear.

Gus takes my hand again, and this time we walk with less worry. We don't want to be assholes, slow walking through New York City, so we decide to stick to the slower sides of the street and get out of people's way. The weather is beautiful tonight, and thankfully my heels aren't killing my feet yet. They might tomorrow, in which case I'll take a gummy before rehearsal.

"Are you open to some dessert?" Gus asks.

"Yes, always." I nod.

"Perfect." Gus looks up at the street signs and then we pivot to turn on the next block.

I don't ask where we're going, just happy to be on this adventure. Gus has a good hold on me, and I admire their hand tattoos over mine. They have a lion on this hand with a huge mane and several other smaller tattoos I can't make out while we walk. I wonder how long they've had tattoos. It must've taken awhile, and it seems like there isn't much of them that isn't tattooed. I blush at the thought of finding out if the tattoos continue everywhere.

"I'm assuming you like ice cream?" Gus asks as we stop in front of a small ice cream shop.

"Yes, I'm not a heathen." I laugh.

Just as we're in line for ice cream, someone taps my shoulder.

"Are you LULY?" The woman is at least eighteen, with a rainbow pin on her jean jacket.

I smile. "Yes."

The woman's eyes widen. "Can I have a picture?"

"Sure." I nod. This was bound to happen; we were tempting fate being out and about without security.

"I can take it," Gus offers.

The girl poses next to me, and we both smile. "My girlfriend is never going to believe this! Your music is an inspiration to us. Thank you so much!"

"Thank you." I smile.

A few more people nearby start to look and realize who I am. Gus shoots me a look and takes my hand. Without speaking, they pull me out of the ice cream shop and we don't stop until we're a few blocks away on an empty street.

TWELVE

Gus

I don't know what actually came over me, but as soon as I saw the look on Emily's face, I knew I needed to get her out of there. One fan we could handle, but a bunch of them and people texting friends to come down isn't something we're equipped for. I knew she was taking a chance when she ditched her security, but I don't want it to end badly. I know the neighborhood, so all I have to do is get her away from the crowds. There are other ice cream shops we can try without her being mobbed by fans. Maybe I shouldn't have listened to her and insisted on security. But I'm not some misogynist who thinks Emily can't fight her own battles. She knows what she can and cannot handle.

"I'm sorry we didn't get ice cream; I can see if there's anywhere nearby," I say once we're alone.

"Are you kidding? I'm sorry we couldn't have any because my fans were around." She laughs.

"Is it always like this?"

"You mean, going out in public and people wanting to have photos and worrying about being mobbed? Yes." She sighs. "It's gotten worse the more famous I've gotten. And I'm grateful for my fans, but it's a lot sometimes. I appreciate you getting me out of there."

"I don't mind; I was just worried about more fans showing up."

"Yeah, it was smart to get me out of there," she agrees.

"There's a bodega on the corner. What do you say we stop in there for some pints of ice cream, and we eat it on the way back to your place?" I suggest.

"Sounds good." She smiles.

We slide in the tiny corner store, stop in front of the two columns of ice cream, and think about which flavors we want. I'm not in the mood for anything crazy, so I grab a plain chocolate while Emily grabs a mint chocolate chip.

"Why are you making that face?" She laughs.

"Isn't eating that the same as eating toothpaste?"

"Uh no, what does your toothpaste taste like?"

"You know what I mean! I hate any kind of mint stuff." I wrinkle my nose.

"More for me." She smiles and hops over to the front counter. She pays for the ice cream against my wishes, and we grab spoons on the way out.

"Which way is your place?" I ask.

"Umm…" She looks around to see where we are. "That way." She points.

I nod, and we pop the lids to our ice cream, tossing them in a nearby garbage can. Emily takes a large scoop of hers and groans when she puts it in her mouth. I've noticed that she's someone who really enjoys food. She doesn't just eat because she has to, she enjoys every flavor. The sounds she makes when she eats are borderline sexual and do something to me. It awakens something in me that I try to ignore.

She licks the spoon clean each time she puts it in her mouth, and I'm like a horny teenager, unable to look away. What the hell was wrong with me? Her pretty pink lips open and her tongue lavishes the spoon. Am I suddenly jealous of a plastic spoon?

Yes. I guess I am. It's because I haven't gotten laid in a while, and I haven't even had any *me* time lately. Everything has been so crazy busy that I'm a little pent up. Clearly, I'll be going home later and doing something about that.

"So, tell me about your day. That's what partners do, right?" Emily says, breaking the silence.

Clearing my throat, I think hard about what she asked me and try to focus my attention on anything but her tongue.

"I went to work, nothing crazy." I shrug as I scoop off a small bit of chocolate ice cream onto my spoon.

"I know, but were there, like, any crazy clients or weird tattoos or anything interesting?"

"Not really. I had a bunch of appointments of people looking to get your lyrics tattooed, by the way. People thought it was cool to get it done by your partner."

"That's so cool; I'm glad this is helping your business. You and River are so talented." Emily smiles.

"Oh! And I had to tattoo this old lady's butt yesterday," I say.

"TELL ME EVERYTHING." Emily laughs.

"Apparently, she bet one of her grandkids that if she lived to be 100, she'd get her butt tattooed. She never thought she'd make it, but she turned 100 yesterday, and her twelve grandkids brought her in. They were cracking up the whole time. I had to get her doctors to sign release forms to make sure it was okay first. She's the oldest person I've ever tattooed," I explain.

"What did she even get?!"

"It said 'bite me' on the side of one of her cheeks." I laughed.

"Oh my God. That's so freaking funny. I hope I'm fun like that someday." Emily smiles.

"Yeah? You wanna get your butt tattooed at 100?"

"Maybe! Or just the fact that I might live to 100 is wild. I hope I'm still having fun then and not just sitting in some nursing home, yelling at the TV." Emily sighs.

"If there even is TV."

"There has to be something for me to yell at." She laughs.

"I realize I never asked, how many tattoos do you have?"

"Just two. River did my first and you did my second. I definitely want more though. I have a Pinterest board full of ideas," she says excitedly.

"That doesn't surprise me; tattoos are often addictive."

"I think of them as being cheaper than therapy." Emily laughs.

"They make you feel better than therapy? That's how I feel about them too," I admit.

"Yeah, it's like a release. I can't explain it more than that, but I always feel like a runner's high after getting one." She smiles.

"That's how I feel too," I admit.

"Who does your tattoos? It's like a doctor needing to go to the doctor. It's weird to ask that." She laughs.

"I did a few of the ones I could reach, but otherwise River did a lot of them. She even recovered up a few I didn't like that much."

"Get an exes name?" Emily nudges me playfully.

"No, just some that didn't age well or faded a lot already. I'm picky about what's on my skin."

"That makes sense."

"What about you? How was your day?" I add, realizing I didn't ask her.

"I had rehearsal for the shows this weekend. It was a lot of repeats of the last week. We're perfecting everything by now, so it's coming along," she explains.

"Well, that's good. I'm excited to see it all in person." I smile.

"Did you ask the girl you like to come?"

"Cari? Yeah, I had River give her the ticket since they're best friends. She texted a thank you and said she'll be there." I honestly forgot all about Cari tonight. She texted me earlier in the day and I don't think I even bothered to respond. Lately it's been like that. It's like I suddenly forgot why I was working so hard to make things good between us.

"Oh, nice," Emily says, but it doesn't sound genuine.

I'm about to ask what's going on with her when we're over-come by a crowd with flashing lights and noise. I drop my ice cream, and Emily's is knocked out of her hand. I immediately grab onto her free hand and try to pull her away from every-thing. It's too chaotic for us to be in the middle of this.

"LULY!"

"LULY! LULY!"

"LULY'S GIRLFRIEND! LOOK HERE!"

"LOOK THIS WAY LULY!"

"SMILE!"

Bright flashes of light are all I can see for a moment while my eyes adjust. There are at least ten paparazzi taking photos of us at once. Emily grips my hand tighter, and I don't let go. If I could see, I'd lead us out of here, but I'm not used to this sort of thing. There are people yelling her stage name, people shouting commands, and fans trying to get selfies in the middle of it all. It's overwhelming to say the least.

"LULY! LULY'S GIRLFRIEND!"

"CAN WE SEE ANOTHER KISS?"

"TWO GIRLS KISSING IS HOT!"

I'm disgusted by the things they're shouting at us, like they've somehow forgotten we're real people. Is this something Emily deals with all the time? I can't imagine trying to have a life if this is what comes with it. Why do people strive to be famous if this is the price you pay for it? Not to mention the fact that they are blatantly ignoring the fact that I'm nonbinary. I thought it was obvious by my non-gender conforming outfits and the way I style my hair and bind my chest. But I guess it isn't obvious if you don't care to look for it. My eyes adjust to the lights, so I try to walk Emily away, but she stands still and looks toward the crowd of photographers.

"First of all, this is my *partner*, Gus. They're not my girlfriend; they use the pronouns they/them. And I'd appreciate it if you could remember that," Emily says angrily. "Take photos all you want, but you won't disrespect my partner by not respecting who they are."

I'm used to being called a girl or people saying she when talking about me. It's something I've learned to ignore; it's usually easier than fighting with people. But no one I've ever dated has stood up for me like this. Making a point to bring up respect and correct them for me. I'm in awe. It's such a small thing that truly means the world to me. Which is probably why I'm not responsible for what happens next.

I pull Emily's body toward mine, letting my hands rest on her hips for just a second. I pull them away to grab her face and kiss her. For a split-second, Emily doesn't move, shocked by the action. But then she moves her lips, and her tongue slips into my mouth. My cheeks heat up with the lights and the way she makes me feel. Her arms find their way around my neck, and I run my fingers through the strands of her blonde curls. I don't know how long we kiss. Our lips never tire of each other's, but eventually we pull back. Emily smiles, the corners of her mouth popping up with the pink hue of her cheeks. She's as flushed as I am.

"Shows over, everyone fan out." Emily starts waving everyone away and they actually listen this time.

I guess they're all running home to be the first to publish that photo of us. I'm sure Emily and I will be making the headlines once again. But this time, it doesn't seem so bad. There will be no denying Emily and my relationship now that we've made it publicly official. Our lips are going to be everywhere, and although that was a little daunting, I don't mind if we are together.

THIRTEEN

Emily

I can still feel Gus's kiss on my lips all throughout rehearsal. Subconsciously, I keep running my fingers over my lips like I'll somehow enhance what I'm feeling. I know we agreed on PDA, and we were in front of the paparazzi, but I didn't see it coming. We were normal one moment and the next they were kissing me with all this passion and lust. We didn't talk about it afterwards. I was too nervous to talk about it, and Gus didn't say a word about it either. Which makes sense; it was essentially a stage kiss. Just two actors playing their respective roles.

"DID YOU SEE?!" Georgie jumps on me in bed this morning.

"No, all I see is my eyelids because I'm sleeping." I groan, trying to push her off me.

"You and Gus made the front page, again!" She holds up my phone in front of my face and I open one eye to peek.

"Huh?" I forgot all about the kiss since I was sleeping, and Georgie was sleeping by the time I got home. But there it is, front and center.

"You guys kissed!? Is that part of the deal, because this looks real as hell." Georgie slides off me and climbs into bed next to me. I'm not wearing any pants, but this is G, and she doesn't care. She wants gossip.

"Yes, we kissed. We talked about it when we made the plan, that PDA to make it look real is okay," I explain, turning over to face her. Her makeup and clothes are already on, even though we don't have to be anywhere for a few more hours. G is a morning person, and I'm often tortured because of it.

"That's disappointing, but I still think they're into you." G shrugs.

"Can I get some sleep? I do have to rehearse later today." I groan. In some ways, I'm glad my best friend doesn't treat me differently for being famous.

"Fine, I'll wake you up in an hour with some breakfast. Eggs?"

"Yes please." I nod.

G places a soft kiss on my head and hops out of my bed and back to the kitchen. I fall back asleep almost instantly. An hour or so later, I'm woken up again, this time with G placing a cup of steaming tea on my nightstand and retreating out quietly. Sitting up in bed, I pull my phone off the charger and brace myself for any messages. Viv left me a voicemail; she was thrilled to see Gus and I on the front page of every social media outlet this morning. Sure enough, the photo *is* everywhere. I can't scroll on my phone without it popping up somewhere. Even Gus sent me a text about it.

GUS: Heard we made the news, guess the kiss will be as memorable as you are

"Lu! Are you okay?" one of the backup dancers asks, and I realize I've been completely lost in thought for too long. I have no clue where we are in the song or what we're up to.

"Sorry, brain fart. Remind me where we are?" I hate being unprepared. I'm trying to break the stereotype that pop stars are conceited airheads.

"First moves of *'Teach Me'*," she says with a soft smile.

"Got it, sorry guys."

I get back into position, and I make sure to stay on task for the rest of rehearsal. I don't even check my phone during breaks because I don't want to get distracted again. Gus is in the forefront of my mind whether I want them there or not. The kiss replays over and over in my head. The way they kissed me left more than a lasting impression on me. I know this is all for the plot, for people to believe that we are together. We were surrounded by the paparazzi, and they had begged for us to kiss. But what confused me was how long they made it last. It would've been believable after a few seconds, but I started to get dizzy from the lack of oxygen.

Viv waves me over at the end of rehearsal, barely looking up from her phone. "Did you talk to your partner about their *schedule*?" she asks, not hiding her disdain.

"They'll be here for the show, and they're free after for any interviews you need. Should I prep them in any way?"

"Nope, it'll be the usual. How did you meet? Are you in love? Are you exclusive? Blah blah. I need to run, but you haven't seen Ken anywhere, have you?" Viv asks, finally looking at me.

"My accounting manager? No, why?" He handles all of my financials, including paying Viv. I check the monthly statements but for the most part, I never hear from him directly.

"Just wondering. I need to have a little chat with him is all." Viv takes off before I can ask any further questions.

"Em!" I spin around, facing Gus being walked onto the stage with security.

"This okay, Miss Ryan? We didn't have them on any list, but we know this is your partner," the security guard says.

"Yes, and please add Gus to the list for the future. It's Augustus Russo for identification purposes," I say.

"Sorry, I just wanted to stop by, I didn't know there would be so many hoops to jump through." Gus chuckles nervously.

I smile, looking at them, a million butterflies appearing in my stomach. Where the hell had those come from? Gus is holding a pink bouquet of flowers and a small pink bag. I don't know what's inside, but I have a feeling it's for me.

"Gus! What a surprise!" Georgie appears out of backstage.

"This is for you, just a little good luck present for tonight." Gus smiles, handing me the flowers and the bag. I breathe in the smell of the flowers; I think they're some kind of daisy. I peek inside the bag and see a box of my favorite chocolates. They're chocolate-covered pomegranates, something I'm always snacking on.

"Thank you so much!" I wrap my arms around Gus. It's a little awkward with so many people around us; I keep trying to remember we have eyes on us.

"It's nothing. My friends are excited for the show tonight."

"You aren't?" I tease.

"Of course, I am. I get to show off my girl and make everyone jealous." They wink.

Georgie shoots me a look, one of those subtle ones that best friends can exchange without even moving their heads. Her look is asking me if I'm seeing this, the fact that Gus is blatantly flirting with me. While mine is telling her to knock it off, because it's all clearly for show. But I didn't ask Gus to show up here with flowers and candy before my show. Is that how they would treat a partner?

"Are you hanging with me backstage tonight, or will you be in the VIP section?" Georgie asks Gus.

"I think the VIP with my friends."

"G, you should join them in the VIP tonight. Their friends are great, and you can actually see the show for once," I say.

"Your friends won't mind?" Georgie looks at Gus.

"Nah, we're always happy to add to our group of misfits. Just be warned, we're all big fans, and some of them are a bit of a LULY groupie. So they might be all over you if they know you're her best friend." Gus chuckles.

"Got it; maybe I'll be a secret double agent tonight," Georgie jokes.

"Lu! Do you have a minute?" my costume designer calls from the side of the stage.

"One second!" I call back. "Can you keep Gus company? I don't know how long I'll be." I look a Georgie.

"Of course, I can tell them all about that time we hitchhiked and saw a psychic," Georgie says with a mischievous smile. I roll my eyes, knowing Georgie won't say a bad word about me. She might tease, but she's harmless. She's probably the only one I trust with my life.

"I'll be back." Without overthinking it, I lean in and kiss Gus's cheek. A brief kiss that leaves behind a small shadow of my pink lip gloss.

I walk over to Ellie, who works for me part time. They run their own fashion line and in their spare time, they create looks for me. They mostly do fashion for plus-size people, but I hired her with the promise that she could recreate my looks for people of any size. She's so talented that I was willing to do anything to hire her. She ties up her long pink curls into a tight, messy bun and leads me to the dressing room. I've seen hints of what she's been creating, and have tried on certain items, but I haven't seen the final things yet.

"Tell me what you hate, and it's gone," Ellie tells me.

"I'm sure none of it will be." I pull out each outfit on the hangers and look at them in awe.

She's perfectly captured my sex appeal, femininity, and boldness into a line. There was an abundance of pink, crop tops, low-cut tops, sparkles, and lace. Of course, I'd have to try everything on, but I can't imagine not looking hot as fuck in everything.

"I had to adjust some of them to be comfortable to dance in, and I was sent an early look of the choreography, so you don't flash anyone… Well, *accidentally*," she adds with a laugh.

"This is so fucking amazing! I'm literally, like, wow. My fans are going to go wild here." I touch everything and smile.

"I know you wanted comfortable yet sexy. The materials are all stretchy and mostly cotton, so you'll be able to breathe," she explains.

"It's actually perfect. Please don't worry, because I don't have a single negative note. Except how the fuck do I choose what to wear tonight?"

"Don't ask me. I saw your girlfriend? Partner? Out there and hot damn. You clearly don't have trouble picking good looking things." Ellie fans herself.

"It's partner, and yes, Gus is hot but that was all by accident. I didn't choose them on purpose, sometimes it's just fate," I say with a shrug. I'm not even lying this time, it was fate. If River hadn't called out sick, she would've done my tattoo, and I'd still be in major trouble with the label.

"Well, then I got nothing. Speaking of hot partners, I need to go. My girlfriend is waiting for me; I think it's our anniversary," Ellie says, checking her phone.

"Go ahead! And don't forget to celebrate, if you know what I mean." I wink at her, and she laughs on her way out.

I glance at all the outfits; there were enough to get me through my commitment to this venue. After the six weeks of shows, I'll be back in the studio to write and record as much of album two as I can. Then the label will be planning my first world tour to celebrate the release of the album. I'm nervous, but this is what I've been working for. So everything with Gus and these shows needs to go perfectly—down to the right outfits for the very first night. I look through the outfits again and realize the perfect one is staring me down. I need something to get the crowd's attention but not show off too much. I needed access to flash everyone—it's my signature move, and I'm not stopping now. Once it's decided, I call the group of fashion assistants to bring the other outfits to holding. Then my hair and makeup team can decide which look will go best with this outfit. I head back to Gus before Georgie asks them if they have a real crush on me.

FOURTEEN

Gus

"So I think I'm supposed to give you the whole 'if you hurt my best friend, I hurt you' speech. But I have a feeling I don't have to worry about that with you," Georgie says when Emily leaves us to talk to someone.

"I definitely won't hurt her," I assure Georgie.

"I figured that. Do you want a tour of backstage? I don't know how long E might be; she's talking to her costume designer," Georgie explains.

"Sure." I nod. I'm a bit out of my depth, but it wouldn't hurt to get a lay of the land. I have a feeling I'll be spending a lot of time hanging out around here.

Georgie leads the way and shows me all the cool spots to hang out backstage. There's a waiting area in the wings where I can hang out and I wouldn't be in the way of anyone. There are several regulars Georgie introduces me to, including Emily's backup dancers, her choreographer, and the sound techs. They're all friendly when they say hello and then get back to what they're doing. I see Viv hanging around, but she doesn't offer anything, not even a friendly wave or somewhat of a smile.

"Is that normal?" I nod toward Viv.

"Viv is… Look, I don't like to speak ill of people, especially E's people. But Viv is not my favorite person. She's a lot and puts a lot of strain on E." Georgie sighs. I must make a face because Georgie quickly catches herself. "I know that's her job, but I just think sometimes she forgets E isn't just a star, she's a person too."

"I see." I already had my own sneaking suspicions about that but with Georgie confirming it, I know I have to be on high alert. Something is off about her, and I don't want to get in the middle of anything, but I also don't want to see Emily get hurt.

"Look, I feel like I can trust you, so don't make it a thing. But just keep an eye out, okay? I'm always on high alert but let me know if you catch something I don't."

"You really have her back. You guys must have been friends for a while."

"We have; we grew up in this small town all the way across America and she's the one who convinced me to come here and follow my dreams. We've been inseparable since we were five." She smiles.

"That's an amazing friendship," I say.

"It's amazing getting to see her have all her dreams come true. She is so talented. I appreciate more than you know that you're *together*." I realize she's alluding to Emily and I's fake relationship without saying it.

"I haven't found it to be a *job* being with her." I wink.

"Got it."

"There y'all are! I've been looking everywhere," Emily says, coming around the corner. "Sorry that took so long, I had to approve the wardrobe choices."

"No worries." Instinctively, I put my arm around her waist and pull her in. I place a small kiss on her hair and Georgie smiles.

"Wait! I should take a photo!" She scrambles to find her phone and grabs a quick photo of us embracing. "I sent it to you, E. Gus, I definitely need your number if we're hanging out in

VIP." Georgie hands me her very pink phone and I type in my number.

"I'll see you two later; I need to get ready for tonight." Georgie says goodbye and I turn toward Emily.

"Hey," she says softly. She seems more shy than usual. I wonder if it's because of the kiss.

"Hey, you excited for tonight?" I ask.

"Yes and no. I know the routine but there's a lot of press and people from the label coming tonight. So I'm just a bit on edge."

"That makes sense. Anything I can do to help?"

"Wanna come smoke a joint with me?" Emily says, and I can't tell if she's joking or not.

"You smoke?"

"Yes, but not often because of my lungs. Sometimes Georgie and I do edibles if it's not a work night," she says. "I take it you don't do drugs."

"Well, I smoked weed a handful of times when I was younger, but I never had a taste for it. I'm happy to grab you snacks if you get the munchies though."

"Nah, I just need to relax. I wish I could take a walk through Central Park without someone seeing me and making it more stressful." She sighs.

I pause, trying to think of something, and I realize something I saw during the tour Georgie gave me.

"So, all the stuff backstage is fair use, right?" I ask.

"Yes, most of it is props we don't use, but if we needed something we could probably borrow it. Why?" She raises a blonde eyebrow.

"Come with me." I take her hand and lead her backstage, trying to recall where I saw it.

I open the room labeled 'storage' and it pops open easily. Inside are tons of costumes, wigs, and makeup.

"What if we didn't look like us? Then no one would follow you, right?"

"Yeah…" I can tell she doesn't know where I'm going with this, so I pick up a bright green wig and hold it over my head.

"If we didn't look like *us*…we could take a walk."

"Oh, my goodness! You're so smart! We could play dress up and go for a walk. Why didn't I think of that?" She laughs.

"I'm sure people might recognize me too, especially if you're dressed up. I don't want anyone thinking I'm cheating on you. So we can both dress up." I look at my watch; we have hours until we have to be back here for her show. Central Park was a good fifteen-minute walk, but it isn't like we are in a rush.

"What are you going to wear?" Emily starts looking through the clothes and I look over the wall of wigs on different mannequins.

"I think we should go for our opposites, so no one even suspects it's us," I say.

"Good idea."

I pick up a fake mustache and hold it over my lip to look in the mirror. I immediately start laughing. I've never considered growing a mustache before. I know it works for some Nonbinary people, but I'm definitely not one of them. I turn to Emily, and she starts cracking up, a loud and boisterous laugh. I relax at the sound.

"You should definitely wear that; no one will recognize you," she says in between laughs.

"Great, I'm going to look ridiculous." I laugh as I start to attach the fake mustache.

"What if I go as an old lady? We can do makeup wrinkles and this grey wig?" Emily asks, holding it up.

"I love it." I nod.

I start looking for something to wear. I really could wear my own clothes, since they are mostly gender neutral, but I don't know if anyone saw me in them today. I decide not to risk it; I find a men's button up and some khaki shorts. I look more like a frat boy than I wanted to, but I'm committed to it, so I grab a snapback too to complete the look.

"Are you cool if I change here?" I ask.

"Uh, sure," she says. She's still looking for old lady clothes so I figure I have a minute.

I tear off the T-shirt I'm wearing and toss it to the side. I adjust my binder to make sure it's on right and then slide on the button up. It fits nicely, which is good because I'm all too used to bigger sizes not fitting like they should be. I change my bottoms but keep my shoes on—they're common enough brand of sneakers that I'm not worried about it. I look in the mirror and tear off the back of the mustache and stick it on my upper lip. Tucking my dark hair into the hat, I laugh as I see myself.

"Oh my God." Emily walks over to see it up close and starts laughing again. "Wait, your shirt is caught... on your bra? Binder? Can I help?"

She looks at my back and I nod. Standing in front of the mirror, I watch as she carefully tries to fix the shirt, but it's not budging from its spot. She slides her hand into my shirt, careful not to touch my skin, and pulls up the fabric to see where it's sticking. I breathe in lightly; I don't know why this feels so intimate. Probably because it's been so long since someone touched me like this. Her face is determined as she looks at my back. I can feel her breath on my bare skin, and I clench my palm on the makeup table in front of us.

"It was stuck on that extra button they always stick to the label. I got it," Emily says, and then carefully fixes my shirt.

"T-thanks." My voice cracks. What the hell was wrong with me? I turn around to face Emily, and just as she looks up, she loses it. It takes me a second to remember the mustache and how fucking ridiculous I look. We both laugh until our stomachs hurt, and I urge her to get ready.

"I think I've got it." She tosses her crop top over her head and my eyes widen as I see her breasts on display. Sure, it isn't the first time I've seen them, and I know she has a habit of showing them at shows. But this isn't a show; this was just the two of us. I spin around quickly before I can think twice about it.

God, why does she have to have such hot boobs? This is not the time to be gay. At least I don't have a dick, or I swear it would be hurting with how hard I'd be in this moment. Emily walks over and I take in her outfit—an oversized purple dress with obnoxious florals and a pair of white flats. She ties up her blonde hair into a ponytail so she can put on the short grey wig. Then she takes an eyebrow pencil and draws wrinkles on her face. When she's done, she's completely unrecognizable.

"So what's our story?" she asks.

"What do you mean?"

"I mean, we're an old lady and a young man walking through the park. Are you my grandkid?" She laughs.

"I'm your lover." I wiggle my eyebrows seductively.

"I can't, okay." She laughs. "I don't know if we're going to make it through the park without laughing."

"So we're a couple who just discovered legal marijuana. You're my old lady," I tease.

We walk out of the storage room, and we get a ton of looks from security. If we weren't on our way out, I think there would be someone stopping us and asking where we were going. Security lets us out, and thankfully I remember my ID, or we might have some issues later. Emily takes my hand, and I'm shocked we don't get any looks on the way to the park. But this was New York, and honestly, as long as you weren't walking slow, you were ignored. No one gives a shit what anyone else is doing in this city.

The streets were crowded because it's a beautiful and sunny day out. So we're dodging tourists who are stopping to stare like they've never seen a building that tall before. Emily and I slip in between people, and a man running with no shirt almost runs into us.

"Hey man! We're walking here!" Emily yells in an old lady voice I'm not expecting. I'm shocked how committed she is to the bit.

"Baby, are you okay?" I ask loudly in a deep voice as I pull her close.

"Oh, hold me, Charlie!" She lays her head on my chest to hide the fact that she's laughing. I press my lips to her hair to hide my own. We get a few looks from on-comers but for the most part, people just pass us by.

FIFTEEN

Emily

"You really don't have time to be hanging out with *fans* before the show." Viv groans.

"Yes, I do. I'm dressed, and we're done with rehearsal. I'm going to see them, and as a reminder these are Gus's friends, so it only solidifies what we're doing here, right?" I remind her.

"Fine." She sighs and angrily waves me off.

I slip past her and bring along security with me. I'm not crazy; sneaking into the VIP section before a show is a little risky. But I want to meet Gus's friends again. I knew how much they mean to them, so I think it is a good next step in our sort of relationship. Not that any of this is real. I don't know why I'm so nervous as I get closer to them. Gus is waiting at the door to backstage, and my stomach is in knots the second I see them. Their hair is slicked back with gel tonight, different than how I saw them just a few hours ago. They're wearing my face on a concert tee, which is actually adorable as fuck.

"Wow. You look amazing." Their jaw drops as they see me. Their eyes rake me over, and I blush as they take their time with my body.

"Thanks, it's a lot more makeup than I usually wear."

"I didn't even notice the makeup. That outfit is going to make every woman in the audience jealous. And the enbies too." They wink.

Fuck, there's that feeling again. Why am I feeling this? I thought I could stick to the rules. It's clear what this is, yet here I am stupidly falling for the one person I know I can't have.

"My friends all made it backstage, but I was afraid they'd ambush you. So I thought it was safer to wait here," Gus explains.

"Thank you. Did Cari come?" I don't know why I sound bitter when I ask. That's part of why all of this is happening. I'm supposed to be helping Gus make her realize what she wants.

"She did."

"Good, we'll have to put on a show then." I reach for Gus's hand and they smile.

We walk toward the VIP box. There are only six fans besides Gus's friends who are there tonight. I'll have to take photos and talk to them too, but I made sure they didn't come through yet. I'll see them after the show for their meet and greet.

"LULY!" River cheers and runs over to hug me as soon as she sees me.

She's wearing this hella cute outfit of ripped fishnet tights and a long T-shirt with my face on it, cut to show off this bright red lingerie she has under it. Her wife, Aspen, is standing behind her with a similar outfit on. She was memorable from her birthday party, but even more so because she was one-half of the very viral, iconic lesbian photoshoot she and River did before they were back together. Those photos were everywhere for months and are still the most searched photoshoot these days. I have to admit, the steam between those two is immense.

"Hey girlie." I smile.

"This is so exciting!" River has been a fan from the beginning, which makes seeing her here an easier experience than meeting one of Gus's friends. "You remember my wife, Aspen."

"Of course. I'm LULY, but you can call me Emily." I shake Aspen's hand.

"This is my best friend, Cari." River introduces a blonde woman with gorgeous curves. Why couldn't she have been ugly? She's wearing bubble braids with glitter sprinkled all over her head and cheeks. Her outfit is similar to River's—a cropped T-shirt of my face and a pair of black leather shorts.

"Hey." I force myself to smile. I don't want to let on to my distaste. It isn't like Cari has done anything; she's just a woman who likes someone. And I'm an idiot with a crush.

"Isla and Rae are supposed to be here…" Gus starts and looks at River for more information.

"They're running late but they did say they should be here by now." River frowns and looks for her phone. Aspen takes it out of her pocket and hands it to her.

"We're here!" a blonde with pink strips of hair says, rushing through to Gus and me.

"Sorry, someone didn't realize that the 1 train isn't running," Says a redhead with gorgeous strawberry curls as she comes up behind her.

"Hey, you could've looked it up!" the blonde argues.

"You said you were handling the transportation," the redhead grumbles.

"Em, this is Isla and Rae. They're the other owners of RARE's tattoos and my friends. Ignore their fighting, that's how they flirt," Gus teases.

"We are not flirting," Rae, the redhead mumbles.

"It's so amazing to meet you. You've made this one smile and that's an accomplishment in itself," Isla says.

"Do you mean Gus is grumpy? I can't imagine." Gus always gives off golden retriever positive energy, so it's hard to see them as someone who could be grumpy.

"Yes, I'm constantly seeing them smiling at their phone like an idiot lately. That has to be you," River adds.

I notice Cari angrily furrows her eyebrows for a moment

before catching herself. I wonder if Gus caught that. Is it possible she's jealous of Gus and I like Gus hoped?

"Any hints on the setlist tonight?" Aspen asks, changing the subject.

"Definitely some crowd favorites, and one or two originals," I say. "But don't tell anyone."

"You know, I can find backstage with my eyes closed, but I had to ask for help to find the VIP lounge," Georgie says with an exasperated sigh.

"Everyone, this is my best friend, Georgie. She's being a showoff because she usually watches from backstage. This is her first time in the VIP seats," I say, smiling at my bestie. A collective hello falls from everyone, and I relax a bit.

I'm glad everyone made it. I only wish Georgie would be able to keep an eye on Gus and Cari for me. But it isn't like I can tell her to. I mean, not without telling her I have a crush on Gus. And that is ridiculous, I don't. I know I don't, I just don't want them flirting or being with anyone else. Yup, I sound nuts, so no way can I say it to anyone, even G.

"Am I totally lame if I ask for some pics with you?" River asks.

"Oh my gosh, of course not! Get over here!" I wave her over and Gus takes the camera.

I take turns taking photos with everyone one by one. Even Cari pops in for a quick photo, and I force a smile. Gus looks like they're going to shit their pants. I don't want to make it a big deal, so I put on my show face. I have a few things to do before the show, so I head backstage with security. I promise to meet up with everyone after the show and after meeting with the fans who actually paid for the other VIP seats. I don't see Viv backstage, but that gives me a second to relax.

Before my makeup artist comes in to work her magic— making me look like I'm not washed out on stage— I look in the mirror. Even though I waxed yesterday and plucked this morning, I have at least four stubborn dark hairs already growing back on my chin. It's one of my least favorite parts of having PCOS. Like, it's bad enough that I have extra body hair everywhere, but these obnoxious and very obvious hairs always appear. I pluck them at home and by the time I'm outside, they are already growing back. Why can't the hair on my head grow that fast? I know, I know, it has something to do with the hormones and having extra testosterone, but it's a pain in my ass.

My makeup team is used to it, and they plucked any I don't see, but I like to make their job easier. So I grab the tweezers and shine my phone light on my face to see if I missed any. The paparazzi are bad enough at blowing them up for the tabloids. I try not to give them any reason to print things about me. Unless it's about Gus and me.

"Lu, are you ready for me?" my makeup artist, AJ, calls through the door.

"Yes!" I call back.

He walks in and sets down his makeup chest on the table in front of me. I take a sip of my water, knowing I'll have to be still until he's done. He always says I can get up if I need to, but I insist on staying still. I don't want to be difficult or hold anyone up. When he is almost done, the hair team will come in and start styling it with way too much gel and hairspray to keep it from falling down. I hate it, but it's better than the alternative of loose hairs falling over my face throughout the entire performance. I usually do the show with a variety of hairdos.

Closing my eyes, I relax into the chair. It's been a long day, and it's only going to get longer. In fifteen minutes, my opening act, a small lesbian band, will be going on. They are still new, but I love their sound. I can see them going the long haul if they stopped hooking up with each other. What is it with lesbians hooking up with everyone and their exes?

"I saw your partner out there tonight; they looked so cute with your face on them," Aj says as he finishes up.

"They always look cute," I say without thinking about it.

"Oh, you've got it baaaaaad." They laugh.

"What can I say?" I deflect. I don't want to deny it, but it's true.

"At least you know they can put up with your fans; those bitches are crazy."

"Oh, they definitely can handle themselves." I smile.

I think about earlier when we walked through Central Park with our disguises. No one suspected a thing, and we were both in hysterics anytime we looked at the other. Gus was my younger, hotter, boyfriend and I was the old lady he was clearly only boning for that paycheck. It was hysterical that we had given our disguises a backstory, but we played it up. When I pulled out my old lady voice, I thought they was going to lose it. I knew I had to commit to the bit; we weren't trying to draw attention to ourselves, but I'm sure we probably looked crazy. Yet, I've never had more fun. It's always like that when I'm with Gus. They are so easy to be with, laugh with, joke with. I know there was no need to have my guard up. They yell at people who bump into us and hold my hand when we cross the street. It's simple, yet so fucking complicated at the same time.

AJ and the hair team finish with me, so I slip into my shoes for the show and drink a few sips of water. I'm not able to drink too much beforehand or I'll have to pee. I get ready to go on, starting the show with my crowd pleaser. I can't see much except the bright lights on me, but I can hear the crowd. It roars with excitement as it sees me, and I transform into LULY.

I'm singing the last line of my favorite song, one of my originals, and I glance toward the VIP section. It's hard to see too far away from me but the lights move, and I look at the fans I don't know. I find Gus's friends, but my eyes search for the one person I want to see right now. I scan the small area until I see Gus being pulled by a blonde. Cari pulls them in for a kiss, and it takes everything in me to keep going. I know what this is; I have no place to be jealous. Yet the sight of Cari and Gus kissing, right in front of me, breaks me right in half.

SIXTEEN

Gus

"Are you kidding me? I didn't know there were snacks here, I only get water backstage." Georgie complains as they bring out a variety of popcorn, candy, hot appetizers, and drinks.

"Do you go to every show?" I ask.

"No, but most of them. It never gets boring; she's just so talented." She smiles.

River starts a conversation with Georgie, so I walk over to the table set up behind the seats that's filled with snacks and drinks. I help myself to a cup of water as Cari comes up behind me. I can smell her vanilla perfume, one of the recognizable parts of her I can't let go of. Cari picks up a bag of Skittles and tears it open with her teeth. She runs her tongue over her bottom lip, something I probably would've found sexy a few weeks ago but now I find anything but.

I hadn't realized it until I saw her again today, but I think I'm over Cari. All the things I used to find irresistible about her are still there, but the feelings of desire no longer are. It's like someone flipped that switch in my brain and in the place it was, there's only Emily. I don't care if Cari is jealous or if she's hanging out with Max later. The only thing I care about these days is if I'm going to see Emily later.

"So, I haven't heard from you lately," Cari says pouting at me. A look that normally makes me putty in her hands. Granted she's still gorgeous; it just doesn't make me feel anything anymore.

"I've been busy, with Emily," I add for good measure.

"You know, that timeline you two are pushing doesn't make much sense. I know for a fact you were with me for a lot of those months you were supposedly seeing her."

"She and I weren't official right away. You know, like how you were seeing Max and me at the same time," I remind her. Cari's face twists and her jaw locks tightly.

"Max! I didn't think you'd make it!" Aspen says, making Cari and I twist around to see Max walking into the VIP space. They hold up their hand shyly and walk over to Aspen.

"Did you invite her?" Cari goes into accusatory mode.

"Do you think if I did, I'd be this surprised to see her?" I scoff. I don't make a habit of bringing my ex's ex places. But I can tell by the look on Cari's face that she didn't invite her either. I guess Aspen invited her; they're best friends after all. I just wish someone had given me a heads up.

Max walks over to us, and I slide back into my seat before she can say anything. I have no problem with Max, but I'm not in the mood to be in the middle of any drama. Tonight is Emily's big night, and I want to make sure we all respect that. The last thing she needs is to look over here mid-performance and see Max and me arguing or Cari and me fighting. I'm going to keep my head down as long as I can. Max and Cari seem to be getting into it but it's all hushed, so I don't really know what's going on. Georgie and River shoot me the same look, which is ironic since they both don't really know what's going on. I just shrug; it isn't like there's anything else I can say.

The concert starts and there's a band I don't know the name of, but they have a really cool sound. River, Rae, Aspen, Isla and

I are getting to know the fans that will be sitting in VIP with us. They have lanyards like us and a meet and greet pass for after the concert. When I introduce myself, two of them go silent as their eyes widen. They both slap the other on the arm and start screaming.

"OH MY GOD! YOU'RE AUGUSTUS! GUS! LULY'S PARTNER! WE'RE OBSESSED WITH YOU!" one of them says.

"Holy shit! You're my background!" The other one says, pulling out their phone to show me proof. There's a photo of Emily and me the first time we kissed as their background.

"Holy fuck, you're famous," Isla whispers in my ear.

"Can we get a photo with you? Our friends will be so jealous!" one of them asks.

"Uh, sure." I nod. I'm still trying to wrap my head around the fact that they have a photo of me and Emily as their background. It's like we're some kind of TV fantasy couple and have had strangers shipping us.

River takes some photos of us and hands the phone back to the girls. "So, how'd you become fans of Gus?"

"We've followed the romance from the beginning. LULY never dates, but when we saw Gus and LULY hugging outside the studio, we knew it was real. We have a tattoo appointment tomorrow to get her lyrics tattooed on us," they say.

"We're hoping she'll write it on our arm so it can be in her handwriting," the other says.

Holy shit, these girls are super fans. I'm a little afraid they might try to take my or Em's blood. I'll have to give security a signal not to leave us alone with them or something. Maybe they're harmless, but I'm starting to air on the side of caution lately. Especially when it comes to Emily.

The opening act ends, so there's a five-minute break where I go pee before Emily comes on stage. When I get back, everyone's in their seats. Which makes me realize the only empty seat was next to...*Cari*. I have a feeling this isn't a coincidence. Max is on the other side, sitting next to Aspen. I guess Cari isn't going to make this easy on herself. Clearly, I underestimated how jealous she would get. My plan with Emily is clearly backfiring and going to blow up in my face soon. I don't know how Emily feels in all of this but I know I'm done trying to make Cari jealous.

"HOW ARE WE DOING TONIGHT, NEW YORK?!" Emily shouts into her bedazzled microphone, and the crowd goes insane. I take my seat next to Cari, but I'm on my feet shouting her stage name.

Emily starts singing and the entire place is singing along. Cari is trying to dance with me, but I subtly ignore her. I'm enjoying my girl's show and that's all I'm going to do. For most of the concert, I manage to ignore Cari. I'm in the zone, singing with Emily, and she's looking over here as much as she can. I don't know if she can actually see me or not, but I have my eyes locked on her. She's flashed the crowd a few times and I thought maybe I'd be jealous, but I'm mostly turned on.

Cari shouts something but I can't hear her that well, so I turn to look at her. She takes my face in her hands and pulls me in for a kiss. For a brief second, I'm reunited with familiarity until I realize what's happening.

"What the hell?" I pull back, eyes wide.

Immediately, I turn my attention to Emily up on stage. At first, I'm sure there's no way she could've seen that, but now I'm not sure. She's been looking over here most of the concert and now she won't even look in this general direction. My attention is quickly back on Cari, who looks shocked that I pulled away from her. Maybe a few months ago I would've been happy with that. A public display and a hint of how she might be feeling about me. But right now? I'm fucking pissed. What the hell is she doing? I shake my head and race away from her.

"Gus!" Cari calls after me and is by my side in seconds.

"What?" I spit. I can't believe she has the audacity to do that, or that she thinks following me is a good idea.

"I-I'm sorry." She's taken aback by my anger. She somehow thought I'd be into that kiss.

"I'm with Emily. I don't know how many fucking times I can say it."

"B-But I thought… you used to want me. You said you'd wait for me," she says firmly.

"I did, and I did wait. But you never chose me, and I moved on. I urge you to do the same," I say angrily.

"I-I thought being with you would make Max jealous. And at first it did, but then you moved on and I didn't know what to do. I thought if I kissed you tonight, I'd get her back. I'm so sorry, I didn't think. I didn't realize how serious you and Emily are."

"Do you not realize how fucked that is? You used me to get someone who will never choose you. You chose someone who will always put you last instead of someone who will put you first and choose you every time. I'm done with your drama, Cari. I don't want it, and you better not have fucked up my relationship with Emily. You need to take a good, hard, look at yourself because honestly, the last thing you should be doing right now is dating." I scoff.

Before she has a chance to reply, I continue from the VIP section to backstage. Emily said my name was everywhere, so I need to get to her first tonight. I don't know if she actually saw what happened or not, but I need to clear things up. I won't keep this from her. I know we've been saying this whole thing isn't real, and maybe at first that was true. But at some point, things changed. Our feelings for each other are real. We need to be together for real. Which means putting all the lies behind us. I can't ignore this.

"Name?" a security guard with a clipboard asks as I reach the entrance to backstage.

"Augustus Russo," I say. He nods and unlocks the door next to him.

I go through the lit path all the way to the side of the stage. I can't remember which side she's going to come out of, but I have a fifty-fifty shot and I need to reach her first. I hang on stage right and try to catch her attention. Maybe if she sees me, she'll come over here regardless. Unless she's so pissed at me that she's going to have me removed. You never really know, it could go either way.

Emily's singing never wavers; the crowd is going wild, and I can just about make out the VIP section from where I am. With all the lights and everything, it might be possible Emily didn't see a thing. Taking that chance, I try to get her attention. Waving from the side of the stage doesn't seem to work so as she stops to take a sip of water, I shout her name. Well, her stage name. She doesn't look, so I call her again, and this time she does. Her eyes widen in surprise and then she goes back to singing. I don't know what it means but at least she knows I'm here.

I can feel my heart beating out of my chest as I wait to face the music. My palms are sweaty as I think about what's to come. Emily doesn't deserve to be cheated on, even if it is a fake relationship. I want to give her everything because she deserves that much. I try to calm my breathing by listening to her sing. I close my eyes and only listen to the lyrics and breathe in and out, only opening them again when I feel better.

SEVENTEEN

Emily

After a show, the only thing I want to do is drink six bottles of water and smoke a blunt. But as I cross into backstage and see Gus waiting for me, I know it's very unlikely I'll get either of those. I'm not surprised to see them backstage. As soon as I saw Cari and them kissing, I figured there would be a conversation. I just figured I had more time before they were going to break up with me. I know we promised to stay together for six months, but I guess they want out. I'm not about to force them to stay or anything. They hand me a bottle of water and follow me into my dressing room. My team is in there, but I ask for the room and they clear out.

"I wanted to talk," Gus starts.

"Go for it." I'm being short, and I know I don't have a leg to stand on, but this sucks.

"I don't know if you saw, but Cari kissed me."

"Oh, I saw." I top off a second bottle of water.

"I had a feeling. But I just want to say—"

"Look, I'll give you an out. If you're done with us, with this" —I motion between us—"then you can have an out. No hard feelings."

"What? That's not what I want." Gus looks at me like I've grown three heads.

"You don't?" I ask, surprised.

"Yeah, I came here to talk to you about it. I know this is…not exactly… but I wanted to explain it. Cari was using me to make someone jealous. And truthfully, even if she wasn't, I don't want her anymore," Gus says.

"Oh," is all I manage to get out.

"You're going to have to give me a little more, because I've been stressing out," Gus says nervously.

"I mean, this isn't, you know, *real*. So I understand if you want to go back to her. I just wasn't expecting you to say you don't want that," I explain.

"Do you want this to be over?" Gus asks.

"What? No. I just thought you did so I didn't want you feeling trapped or anything," I say.

"I don't feel trapped."

"Okay, cool. I know you've sort of lost your motivation behind this, so if you want the money or anything just let me know," I tell them.

"No, I'm still in this. And I don't want the money."

"Okay."

"Em—"

"Sorry to interrupt, but we need to get you to the VIP meet and greet now," one of Viv's assistants says, opening the door slightly.

"Sure." I nod and stand.

"We'll talk later?" Gus asks.

"I'm probably going to be busy with work all night…"

The assistant interrupts, "Actually, Viv said I was supposed to get both of you. She said you have interviews in the green room afterward with the press."

"Oh shit, yeah." I nod. I had completely forgotten.

"I'll be there," Gus says, and I nod.

They follow me out of the dressing room, and we go down

the hall to the VIP room with the assistant. I don't want to do this tonight. I'm in a bitter mood after seeing Gus kiss someone else. I know I have no right, and I'm doing everything I can to deny it, but it's clear I have feelings for them. Feelings I needed to bury deep down if I'm going to keep this fake relationship going. For the sake of my career, I can't let my feelings get in the way. It's what is best for everyone. Gus and I are just friends faking it.

I put on a face as I greet everyone in the VIP room. It's mainly Gus's friends and a handful of actual fans, and I don't have to fake it with the latter. They genuinely make me happy; I mean, they are the reason I have a career. I take photos, sign things, and answer questions. Two girls even ask me to write lyrics on their arm that Gus is going to tattoo on them tomorrow. It doesn't get more surreal than that.

When I get to seeing Gus's friends again, I realize Cari is nowhere to be found. Thankfully, no one mentions it, and I don't ask. I'll have to find out everything from Georgie later. She was there and I know she will tell me the truth. As we slide through the end of the meet and greet, Gus and I are ushered into the green room. It's basically a fancy conference room with an oval table filled with media types. Social media influencers, newspaper and magazine reporters, along with podcast hosts. Gus takes a seat next to me and takes my hand.

I see Viv in the corner reminding me to smile and pushing the questions in certain directions. She wants me to be in the press for more than my tits, which I understand, but a lot of this feels fake. It's one thing for my relationship to be, but I hate not being able to be myself when it comes to answering questions for the press. I want my fans to see an authentic version of myself. So halfway through, I stop looking at her and start answering for myself. It feels more genuine and less rehearsed. I can tell Viv is freaking out, and I might have to deal with the repercussions of that later, but for now I don't care.

"That's all the time we have folks." Viv dismisses everyone and tells Gus and me to stay behind.

"What the hell was that?" Viv screeches as she shuts the door behind her.

"What?" I play stupid.

"You know what. Those were not the answers we went over," she snaps.

"I wanted to be myself; I want my fans to see me. Not some watered-down version of me," I say.

"That's not what—"

Gus cuts Viv off. "I'm sorry, but what's the harm in that? Emily sounds like herself instead of some rehearsed bullshit version of herself. As a fan, it makes her seem more real."

"First of all, you're only in here because I let you be. Don't make me regret that. Second of all, we tested these responses with the team. They're responses to get Emily's career back on track," Viv says angrily.

"I appreciate that, but I'm not going to fully change who I am just to keep my fans. They like me because I'm me," I say firmly.

"You're so naive." Viv scoffs and leaves with a shake of her head.

"Do you have anything else to do tonight?" Gus asks.

"Not really, I just want to change and head home though. I'm sorry, I'm always exhausted after a show." I sigh.

"No worries at all, I think my friends are going out, but I have work tomorrow."

"I'll see you tomorrow night then or?"

"Yeah, you have a show, right? I'll be out of work by then." They nod.

"Thank you for today." I smile. "And thank you for telling me about…everything. It's better there's no surprises."

Gus nods and they walk me back to the dressing room. They grab their stuff, and I head to the bathroom to pee. Those three water bottles I had went right through me. I sit and pee, but the second I stand, I start to feel dizzy. My face gets hot, starting with a small sweat that breaks out all over my body. Am I getting a fever or something? I splash some cool water on my face, but it doesn't seem to help. I feel a sharp stab into my lower abdomen. It's like someone stabbed me with a sharp knife and quickly took it out of me. I groan in pain; I wasn't expecting that. What the hell is going on? What side is your appendix on? Uh, the right, I think. But this is from the left side. At least there is no chance I'm pregnant and didn't know it or something. My heart starts beating faster and my vision gets blurrier. I grip the sides of the sink but then my vision gets smaller. It goes from just the corners of my eyes to everything going black.

The next thing I hear is Gus's voice. "Em, it's going to be alright."

I open my eyes and see Gus sitting next to me in what looks like an ambulance. What happened? The last thing I remember is being in the bathroom, and things got blurry. I must've passed out. I register the oxygen mask on my face and move it to talk.

"Oh God Em, thank God." Gus sounds so relieved.

"Did I pass out?" I ask hoarsely.

"Yes. Ma'am, do you remember what happened?" the EMT asks.

"I had a sharp pain on my left side. Like a stabbing, I overheated and then everything went blurry," I say.

"Okay, has this ever happened before?" they ask.

"No." I shake my head. I feel okay now; was I just dehydrated?

We get to the hospital, and they rush me to a private room. I'd cause too much commotion just being in the emergency room. A doctor and a nurse run a variety of tests, sending Gus to the waiting room. I answer too many questions and while they wait for tests, I ask for Gus and my phone. Of course, no one grabbed that, so I ask Gus to borrow theirs.

"I already texted Georgie if that's what you need. She's on her way. I think she's taking an Uber," Gus says, and I freeze.

"You called Georgie?"

"Uh, yeah? I'm sorry, I sort of assumed that would be your emergency contact. I thought she'd want to know either way," Gus says nervously.

"Thank you. That's right, she is." I smile. It's nice that Gus thought of that.

"Okay, so we have the test results. Is it okay to talk in front of your…" the doctor says, eyeing Gus. Just as Gus goes to leave the room, I grab their hand tightly.

"My friend, you can talk," I say.

"So you passed out due to the pain. It seems like you had an ovarian cyst. It's very likely that the cyst burst and due to its size, you felt it. We gave you Tylenol for the pain. It says in your chart that you have PCOS; are you taking anything for that?" the doctor asks and I sigh a breath of relief. I've had cysts before, but I've never had burst before. I'm glad it wasn't something else.

"I'm not. I was on birth control for a little while, but it raised my blood pressure. I did go gluten free for my symptoms, and it helps," I explain.

"Got it," the doctor says.

"There wasn't any damage, right?" Gus asks.

"Nope, it will pass on its own. We think it's due to your strenuous dancing on stage. It might've shaken your insides around. We recommend rest for the next few days, and if you feel any worse or pass out again, definitely come back," the doctor says.

"Okay," Gus and I say in unison.

The doctor leaves, and they send Viv in with my approval. She stops when she realizes Gus is here and then smiles.

"You have no idea how good this will look for the press." Viv smiles proudly and pulls out her phone to start typing.

"What?" Gus's jaw ticks.

"There's a photo of you getting into the ambulance with Emily that is going viral. Someone from TMZ was there because of the concert and caught everything," Viv explains.

"You've got to be kidding me." Gus scoffs and I look at them, confused.

"What?" Viv breaks contact with her phone for a split second to look at Gus.

"You walk in and the first thing you say is how good this will look for the press? I found her passed out in her dressing room. Not a simple 'I'm relieved you're okay'? I don't understand how you can work for someone and not give a damn about who she is as a human being," Gus lets out angrily and storms out of the room. My jaw drops. I know Viv is bad but I've never had anyone stand up for me like that. I'm so used to Viv but that doesn't mean it's okay.

"You've got to control her. There's no way this will end well if she doesn't rein herself in." Viv scoffs, going back to her phone.

I feel the blood rise to my head. "They. They are not a she." I growl. "I want you to go, and if you see Gus, please send them back in."

"Fine." Viv leaves with a roll of her eyes.

EIGHTEEN

Gus

"Whoa, whoa, whoa. Are you okay?" Georgie stops me in my tracks.

"Sorry, I just… Viv just pissed me off and I needed to get out of there before I said something worse." I sigh. Georgie raises an eyebrow, and I explain what happened. It isn't like she's going to have a different reaction than I had.

"But E is okay? I was so worried." Georgie breathes a sigh of relief.

"Yeah, she just has to take it easy for a few days."

"I'll be around tomorrow, but shit, I have work on Monday. I'm starting a new project, and I really can't afford to call out. Maybe I'll call her mom to come in." Georgie starts thinking.

"I can stay with her," I say.

"Oh, duh, I didn't think of that. Don't you have work?"

"I do, but I co-own the studio. I can afford a few days off. I can come by Monday morning with breakfast," I suggest.

"That would be perfect." She smiles.

Viv passes us by and we glare at her as she walks by. We both head into Emily's room and she smiles when she sees us. I'm glad to see her smiling. I didn't know it, but finding someone passed out might be the scariest thing I've ever felt. I went back to talk to her, thinking maybe now was the time to tell her about my feelings. But when I opened the door, she was on the floor between the bathroom and dressing room. I rushed to her and when she didn't answer, I called for help and 911. Viv freaked out when she ran in, but she never once asked about her. She was freaking out to an assistant about what this was going to look like.

"The doctor said I can come home tonight; they're going to get the paperwork done." Emily smiles.

"I'll be home to take care of you tomorrow all day, and Gus is going to stay with you when I'm at work this week," Georgie tells her.

"I don't need a babysitter. I'm totally fine." Emily laughs.

"Yes, you do. You passed out and were all alone. If Gus didn't find you today, it could've been really bad. So you're going to let us stay with you," Georgie says firmly, as a parent would tell a child.

"It was really terrifying finding you like that," I say quietly.

She sighs. "Fine, if you guys want to spend all your time with me like some kind of stalkers, who am I to judge?" We both start laughing at her joke.

After filling out a boatload of paperwork, Georgie and Emily load into her car and head for home. I promise to check in with them tomorrow, and Georgie says she'll send their information over. I head home for the night and only relax the moment my head hits the pillow. I had too much on my mind, so I'm glad to get some sleep.

In the morning, I feel like I'm on routine mode. I'm going through the motions but all I am is worried about Emily. I know logically that she's okay and if something happens, Georgie will call me. But finding her last night is still fresh in my mind. I've never really worried about things like that before. I have anxiety like most people, but it's more about getting pushed on the Subway tracks or a gunman somewhere thanks to our country's lack of gun laws. So to be reminded that people aren't indestructible, it rocks you a little.

I get through most of my day in silence until I reach the girls from last night. They come in with their arms ready to be tattooed with Emily's words and they are in hysterics.

"I didn't know if you'd be in today! We saw her get taken away!"

"We were so worried!" they both exclaim.

"She's okay now," I say. I'm not trying to divulge too much to anyone. It isn't my place to share her medical news.

"Is she home? She cancelled her tour dates for the rest of the week!"

"She's been instructed to rest and when she feels better, she'll be back to work," I say reassuringly. I don't want anyone starting rumors about where she might be or what's wrong with her. And she definitely isn't cancelling the rest of her tour; she just needs to take it easy this week.

It seems to satisfy them, and they realize they will not be getting much out of me. By the time I'm done tattooing them, I realize it's time to head home. I pop my head in River's office before I go.

"I got something for LU-Emily. We all wanted to chip in, but we hoped you could give it to her?" River pulls out a small basket and hands it to me.

"What's in it?" I ask.

"A spa treatment gift card to the place Aspen and I like to go, a romance novel about a lesbian singer, some lotions and face masks, and a gift card for DoorDash. We didn't know what she likes to eat or if she's allergic to anything so we figured that was the way to go food wise." River smiles.

"That's so thoughtful, thank you. I'm sure she'll love it."

"I'm not asking to be nosey, and it'll stay between us, but is she okay?" I know River is asking from a place of care but I don't want to risk it so I just nod.

"It's not my place to say more. But yeah, she's okay. And I

appreciate the time off this week; Georgie and I don't want her to be alone," I explain.

"No worries, if there's anything I can do when you're out let me know. I hope she gets better." River smiles and I head out for the night.

In the morning, I'm up at the crack of dawn; no like, literally at six a.m. It's so early, it's still dark outside until after I'm done with my shower. I still don't know why people get up this early every day, or by choice. But I have a mission to get a few things done before I'm expected at Emily's house at 9 a.m. Georgie leaves for work then, and I need to be there so she can let me in. She texted last night saying it was probable Emily would still be sleeping when I get there. She isn't a morning person either, I guess. So Georgie will let me in and I'll hang out in the living room until Emily gets up. Emily and Georgie agree that if I don't hear her breathing or see a sign of life by noon, I'm to go in her bedroom and check on her.

But before I get to that, I stop at the gluten-free bagel place I found online last night. It's on the Upper West side, which of course isn't on my way to Em's at all. But I want to bring her something I know she will eat. I also stop at the drugstore nearby to grab a few random things. Muscle cream, extra strength Tylenol, electrolyte drink, and her favorite candy. I did some googling since her cyst ruptured and there isn't much I can do, but if she's sore or hurting, I'll be prepared.

The scary thing the internet said is this is a common symptom. I don't know much about PCOS; I have my own thoughts about having a uterus. I'll eventually get mine removed but it's on the list of things I'll do when I don't hate going to the doctor. But to know Emily's was punishing her in all these ways I didn't realize feels shitty. She can get cysts at any time, and they can just burst like last night or go away on their own. They can also get large enough to need surgery, but for the most part there isn't much you can do.

I'm at Emily's apartment by 8:55 a.m. with my ID in hand to show the front desk. It's a fancy building and Georgie says the security is tight. Once my ID clears and they buzz Georgie to say I'm here, I'm escorted to an elevator. I'm not allowed to touch the buttons myself, and I have a feeling this person will stay with me until Georgie invites me in. Personally, I love all the extra measures in place to keep them safe.

"You're right on time, Emily's still sleeping. I usually make her a cup of tea if I want her to get up. She's not taking pain medicine or anything, but she's been sleeping a lot. Her door is cracked so you can listen in to make sure she's like, alive. I'm going to peek in and let her know you're here," Georgie says as she puts on an earring after answering the door.

"Got it. I brought bagels—Gluten-free but I swear they taste the same," I say. I was too hungry on the train not to try one. I'm actually impressed at the quality.

"She's going to love that. You can set it on the counter. If you need the fridge for anything, go ahead. The bathroom is down the hall to the left, by the way, and her bedroom is to the right," Georgie says before disappearing down the hall.

I can hear her whispering to someone as I set the bagels down. I don't want the cream cheese going bad, so I put it in the fridge and wash my hands. Georgie comes out five minutes later in a different outfit with a bag on her shoulder.

"Call me if you need anything. Work knows I'll have my phone on." She smiles. "I feel like I'm leaving my kid with a nanny or something." She laughs.

"Don't worry, I know the poison control number and CPR," I joke.

"You do?" She looks surprised.

"A lot of people pass out when getting tattoos. I've only had to use it once, but it's a good skill to have." I shrug.

Georgie nods and slips on her shoes before I lock the door behind her.

Heading down the hall, I investigate where Emily's room is. I can hear her breathing and snoring lightly, so I relax a bit. It feels weird being in someone else's home when they were asleep, but it isn't like I can do anything. Georgie and I know Emily doesn't need anyone watching her. But we also both care about her too much to leave her alone right now. And Emily knows better than to argue with us. So I plop on the couch and scroll on my phone for a bit. I have my iPad with me too, in case I want to draw any tattoos. I can check the schedule and see if I have any custom appointments coming up and get ahead.

"Good morning; sorry I look like a bum." Emily waves coming around the corner.

She's wearing a long pink robe that falls to the floor; it looks cottony and fluffy. Her hair is in a mess on top of her head, somehow still in the same hairstyle as the other night. She's only wearing a long T-shirt under the robe, with the possibility of wearing tiny shorts. It's the first time I'm seeing her without any makeup, but you'd never know it. She looks just as beautiful as she always does. The only difference is her usual smile and radiance are replaced by sleepiness. She rubs her eyes, and I smile.

"You look beautiful."

"I swear I've showered since I've seen you. But my hair had so much gunk from the show, and I didn't have the muscle strength to clean it, so I've left it." She groans.

"You're totally fine. I'm not worried about your hair, I'm just glad you're okay."

NINETEEN

Emily

I feel like shit until the moment Gus looks at me. The way their face changes as I walk into the room is enough to induce butterflies. I know I look like shit; I saw myself in the mirror just now. But Gus is looking at me like I just walked off a runway, and I'm flattered. Georgie is gone for work, and I don't want to sleep the whole day away. I'll eventually have to get back in a routine, so I figure waking up for breakfast was a good first step.

"I got you gluten-free bagels. They're on the counter. Do you want me to make you one?" Gus asks, standing.

"Nah, I can do it." I wave them off and make my way into the kitchen. The floor is cold on my bare feet, but I have slippers around here somewhere.

"Georgie said you might want tea, but then didn't show me where it is."

"I can get that too, I swear. I am fine, just tired, but I'm not going to pass out or anything. They said that was a fluke and I don't need anyone waiting on me," I say firmly.

"Okay." Gus nods and takes a seat at the couch again.

"What is it?" I ask Gus, noticing the small basket next to the bag of bagels.

"Oh, my friends were worried about you, they asked me to bring it."

"What's in it?" I peek inside to see what it is.

"A spa treatment gift card, a romance novel about lesbians, some lotions and face masks, and a gift card for DoorDash. They didn't know what you like to eat but wanted you to be able to get food," they say.

"Wow, that's so kind."

I glance at the table full of gift baskets. Most are from my team and the label, all hoping I get better soon. They're generic, clearly pre-packaged baskets that took longer to add their credit card numbers in than pick what I'd actually like and use. How did Gus's friends, who met me all of one time, know me better than people who are around me all the time? Even Viv's basket has a box of cookies and crackers that aren't gluten-free. Something I know she knows about me but doesn't bother to worry about. My eyes start to water.

"Shit, are you okay?" Gus rushes to my side and hands me the box of tissues.

"I'm sorry, it's just your friends are so kind. And you too, like you remembered I'm gluten free and went out of your way to get me bagels I can actually eat. It's a small gesture but it really means a lot. I have Georgie, but besides that there isn't anyone else going out of their way for me unless they're hired to." I sob lightly.

"Hey, it's okay." Gus pulls me in for a hug. Not too tight to squeeze me, but they hold me firmly against them. They rub my back with one hand and hold the back of my head with the other.

"I'm sorry. I've been a little emotional about all this," I admit. I was terrified that I actually passed out on my own.

"It's completely understandable," Gus whispers.

I let it out into Gus's chest, sobbing lightly until I feel better. Gus rubs my back and stays quiet until I pull away. We both look at Gus's chest, wet from my tears.

"Guess I gotta wash my shirt, unless you need it tonight for a tissue?" Gus teases and I laugh. I know they don't care about the shirt and are happy to have helped.

"Maybe I will take you up on that help. Can you toast me a bagel while I shower? I think I wanna wash my hair." I sigh.

"Of course. Just take your phone in case you need help," Gus says, and I nod.

I head to the bathroom, strip down to nothing, and turn on the water. I turn it all the way up so there's steam invading the entire room. The bathroom door is cracked in case I get dizzy or need help. Not that I want Gus seeing me naked for the first time to be like this. Not that I think about Gus seeing me… suddenly I feel flushed. Why am I having dirty thoughts about Gus? I know where the two of us stand. Yet the way they look at me and held me, not to mention that kiss?

I slide into the shower and close the curtain behind me. I hesitate only for a second and slip my hand down my center. Brushing my fingers over my clit, I can feel how it's already sensitive and swollen. My fingers slip further down my folds and are soaked instantly. Damn, there is no hiding what Gus does to me. But this is fine; it will stay between me and the shower. As long as I'm quiet. Although the thought of Gus hearing me and joining me in here do add fuel to the fire. I mean, how could it not?

My nipples harden as the water hits them, and I close my eyes and relax. My fingers dance across my clit and I bite down on my lip to hold back a moan. The feel of Gus's lips on my body plays in my head. Their body pulled against mine, the friction and tension driving us wild. I can feel my orgasm building and just as it does, I also start to feel dizzy. My hand snaps back as my eyes shoot open. The last thing I want is Gus finding me naked and passed out from an orgasm about them. Talk about mortifying. I don't think I'd ever recover from something like that. So although it leaves me unsatisfied, I finish my shower without finishing myself.

Scrubbing my head clean, I add extra leave-in conditioner. It will be a pain and a half brushing it, but I will manage. When I get out, I change into a pair of sweats and a crop top. I'm not forcing myself to wear a bra. It isn't like Gus hasn't seen my tits before. It just doesn't help that every time I see them, my nipples get hard.

Gus is waiting for me back on the couch. A cup of steaming tea in a mug and my bagel with cream cheese wait on the coffee table. I take a seat next to Gus and sigh.

"I swear this is the last thing I'll ask for, but could you help me brush my hair? I don't wanna get the knots out myself," I admit.

"Of course." They nod, taking the pink brush from me.

I sit on the edge of the couch, and they sit to the side of me. Taking a handful of my wet, blonde hair, they start to brush gently. I don't think they'll get many knots out that way, but somehow, it's working. Gus takes their time in each section until it's easy to swipe the brush through. I take bites of my bagel as they work, and I'm impressed. I need to get the name of this bagel place, for sure. Gus's hands are soft and tactile as they run through my hair. I can feel the warmth of their palms as they brush out each knot. It's euphoric, the way they work meticulously.

"I think I got them all," Gus says as they finish. I touch my hair, and it feels brand new.

"Thank you." I smile.

Gus nods and puts the brush on the coffee table. I finish my last bite of bagel and have a sip of my now lukewarm tea. It's just sweet enough, exactly as I like it. Knowing Georgie, she probably made a video instruction manual of how to make it the way I like.

"Do you wanna watch a movie or something?" Gus asks.

"Maybe we can listen to some music?" I suggest. I'm kind of tired and I don't think I can stay awake for a whole movie.

"Sure, do you want me to play something on my phone?" they ask, raising an eyebrow at me.

"No, I have a record player. You can look through my album collection. I have more but they're in storage for now." I point to the wall full of records and the player on display on its shelf.

"Got it." Gus nods and looks through the albums carefully.

I know I don't need to worry, Gus handles everything with care. They choose one, take it out of its sleeve, and place it on the turntable. I relax as the familiar song fills the air. I haven't listened to this one in a while but it is an old favorite of mine.

"I'm shocked you have this; it's my favorite song" Gus admits.

"This is your favorite song?!" I gasp. "Lovefool" by The Cardigans is not a common song by any means, and it definitely doesn't seem like Gus's typical music.

"Yeah, it's like, vintage and cute. I don't know why but it always puts me in a good mood." They smile.

"That's how I feel too."

Gus sits back down, and I move a little closer. I'm inching over when Gus pulls me into their arms. They wrap one arm around my shoulders and tap their other hand on the arm of the couch, and I feel relaxed. I ease into the music and shut my eyes. I can smell Gus's scent, some kind of perfume/cologne that smells more outdoorsy than you'd expect. It's elegant with some sort of beach vibe. Gus taps along with the song, even humming, and I sing along quietly. I don't like singing when I'm not on stage. I'm always worried it won't sound good or people will start to ask for requests like I'm some DJ. But instead, Gus gets quiet and lets me sing. I know I don't need to keep going, but I want to. The song repeats itself and I slowly drift into sleep.

When I wake, the record player is still playing the song. Gus is twirling my blonde hair around their thumb and pointer finger. My eyes flutter open and Gus is looking down at me with dark brown eyes. I've seen them before, but the way they look at me feels more intimate than before.

I start to wonder if this is starting to feel more real to them too. Maybe it isn't in my head, and we aren't just faking things anymore. Maybe Gus and I actually are *something*. I mentally shake my head; I can't let my feelings run wild just because they took care of me when I was sick. They're a good friend, a great friend, but that is all. The keyword there was *friend*. I should know better than to get involved with someone I can't avoid. It isn't like if I told Gus how I feel and they don't feel the same that we can go our separate ways. And I don't even want that anymore. We've grown to be there for each other. My days feel better when I talk to them. I can't imagine having to give that up if I go and ruin it all.

"Sleep good?" Gus asks, noticing I'm awake.

"Mmm." I nod. "What time is it?"

"Just after one, you slept about two hours," Gus says, looking at their watch.

"Why didn't you wake me? I'm sorry." I rush to get off their lap, but Gus stops me.

"It's okay, I'm glad you got a nice nap," they reassure me.

I sit up and look at the cup of tea that has now definitely gone cold. Gus stretches their arm as I move off it and I wait for the feelings to leave. For the butterflies to fly back home. To not feel the way I do in this moment. But as Gus looks at me with soft, kind eyes, the butterflies set up camp for their new home.

TWENTY

Gus

Two weeks after Emily's scare, everything is back to normal. She only had to cancel one show, and she was back on stage for the next performance scheduled. She even made sure everyone who missed her show was given VIP tickets for any upcoming show they could make it to. The only downfall was we didn't have much time to be alone since then. Viv was constantly having us do press and interviews about how her time off was good for our relationship. I was even given things I was supposed to say instead of leaving everything to Emily. It was a little chaotic, but I was glad things were getting back to normal. So when Emily asks to hang out tonight, I say yes without thinking about it.

EMILY: I was thinking we could try this new Thai place?

ME: What if we didn't go out?

EMILY: like you want to cancel tonight?

ME: No, like what if we order in food instead?

EMILY: You wanna come over?

ME: What if you come to my place and I'll order you dinner?

EMILY: Sounds good to me

. . .

I text her my address and she lets me know she'll be over soon. I quickly clean up my apartment for company. Hiding all my dirty clothes in the laundry bin, cleaning three-day old dishes, and putting away the dildo in my bathroom. I definitely don't want to explain that to Emily. Sure, she and I flirt, but ever since that night, things have been different between us. Like we aren't quite sure where we stand anymore. We do a lot of couple things when we don't need to be. Like when there's no chance of someone seeing us. And we've been spending a lot of time indoors, which is the opposite of how this started.

"Bitsy, Sparks, Cat Burglar!" I call out, knowing they will be hiding when Emily comes over. They are shy at first, so I want to make sure they eat their dinner before she gets here.

They all come out of my bedroom and stop in the kitchen next to their bowls. They must've heard me open the cans of food. I plop a bit of food in their bowls and then go back to cleaning up around the place. Cat Burglar knocks over his bowl and I hear the clang as it hits the floor. I turn around and stare at him like a mother displeased with their toddler.

"Dude, why can't you just leave it there? I know when you're done, you don't need to knock it over and make a mess." I sigh and walk over to clean it up. Thankfully, he was done so there isn't food all over the floor under it.

"Emily is coming over guys. I really like her, and I think you'll like her too. She's very pretty and talented and she's my girlfriend, but I want her to be my girlfriend for real now. I know that doesn't make sense, but it's complicated." I continue on, explaining my confusing love life to my cats. They sit near me as I clean. Perched on their back legs, they look like they're listening intently. Except Cat Burglar, who is off in the living room climbing on the back of the couch.

"Thank you both for not getting into trouble like your brother," I tell Bitsy and Sparks as I pick up Cat Burglar off the edge of the sofa and put him on the floor.

A notification on my Ring camera lets me know Emily's here, and I head downstairs to let her in. It's an old building and the buzzer is a bit temperamental, but at least there is an elevator. When I get to her, she's smiling behind a baseball cap and sunglasses, her signature in-hiding look. Quickly, I let her in and lead her to the elevator.

"Your building is so nice! Holy shit, your apartment is nicer than mine!" Emily gushes as she walks inside.

"It's not but thank you." I laugh.

"It really is, look at this amazing view. You can see the Brooklyn Bridge from here!" she says, standing in front of my huge living room windows.

"It's also rent controlled." I like to brag about that whenever I can.

"Now I hate you. We should've signed a prenup in this arrangement so I could get this place," she jokes.

"I think that would only work if we broke up," I remind her.

"Darn, then I guess I'm out of luck either way." She laughs.

"How are you feeling?"

"Good, totally back to normal. My doctor wants to do monthly scans for cysts so we can see before one bursts. But I'm okay for now," she says proudly.

"That's awesome."

"So how come you didn't want to go out tonight?"

"I had a long day, and I wanted to enjoy a night in. Like, a more relaxing night than possibly getting chased by paparazzi or crazy fans," I admit.

"I'm sorry. I know how that is." She sighs but I take her hand.

"No, I get it. It's just nice sometimes when we can get away from it." I smile.

I'd be lying if I said there weren't ulterior motives for inviting her over. I've been searching for the right moment to talk to her about how I feel. Even if it is awkward or she doesn't feel the same, I think I owe it to myself to at least tell her how I feel. It seems like there is something real happening between us and I want to know if it is all in my head or not. Emily and I take a seat on the couch, and I try to figure out the best way to approach this.

"Oh my gosh! Do you have cats?!" Emily asks excitedly as her attention turns behind me.

"Yeah, the black one is Bitsy. The one with white spots is Sparks, and Cat Burglar is around here somewhere. He's orange, so you can't miss him," I explain.

"They are adorable! Are they friendly?" Emily asks, sitting on the floor near them.

"Truthfully, they're usually shy at first, so I'm shocked they're even out right now," I admit.

"Hello," Emily says in a baby voice to Bitsy and holds out her hand.

Both cats walk over and sniff it before deciding they like her and rubbing their side along her legs. Emily pets their bodies as they each lay on either side of her and I watch in amazement. It took Kenzie months for them to warm up to her like this. I was shocked they were so warm and welcoming. I guess it's because they can tell I trust and like her? The real test will be Cat Burglar, he is the most temperamental of the bunch.

"Oh my goodness, he's so pretty!" Emily says as Cat Burglar comes out of the bedroom. Probably because the others are purring under Emily's touch.

"He's not as friendly as the others, so just beware," I tell her.

But of course, he does the opposite and goes right up to her, rubbing his back along her back and looks up at me like I'm some kind of a liar. Of course he does. I toss my hands in the air in defeat.

"Clearly they like me." Emily laughs.

"Well, I've had them for years and I can say they aren't like this with anyone else."

"I'm very much a cat person. I want to get one, but Georgie is allergic." She sighs.

"Well, you can come visit them anytime you want." I smile.

She looks back at me, beaming, a smile as big as her face. Sitting with my cats, she looks relaxed as can be. Eventually they decide they've had enough and leave to sit in their spots by the window to soak in the last bit of the sun. It's summer, so the sunset is still late in the day. Emily takes a seat next to me on the couch and I look at her. Blonde hair tightly wound in a ponytail, a pink T-shirt with her slogan on it, and sweatpants that hide curves I know she has. She is so gorgeous without even trying.

"Why does your face look like that? Do you have to poop?" Emily asks and we both start laughing.

"No." I playfully shove her arm, and she relaxes.

"I thought I'd have a better way of saying this, but I guess I'll just say it."

"If you're trying to break up with me, I swear I'm going to hit you with this pillow," Emily says, eyeing the throw pillow next to me.

"No, just the opposite, actually." I rub the back of my head awkwardly.

"What?" She looks at me, confused.

"I don't want this to be fake anymore. I want a chance to be your real partner," I say quickly.

Emily's face is unreadable. I have no idea if she's trying to think of a way to let me down gently or tell me she loves me.

"Okay." Emily nods.

"Okay?" I'm going to need a little more of a response than that from her.

"I-I like you too. But I never would've had the guts to say it. I thought you were ending this and that's why you wanted me to come over." Emily laughs nervously.

"You like me too?" I relax a little as I repeat her words.

"Yes, but I wasn't sure you felt the same." Emily picks at the fuzz on the pillow and avoids eye contact with me. I tilt their chin up to look at me.

"Can I kiss you?" I know we'd kissed before, but this is different, and I want to be sure this is what she wants.

"Yes." She smiles and her cheeks turn pink.

Leaning in, I slowly press my lips to hers and we both smile. Trying again, I keep my eyes shut as I kiss her, soft lips disappear into mine. Holding her face in my hands, I feel her cheeks warming up. My heartbeat quickens as she slips her tongue in my mouth. Mine tangles with hers, and it becomes a mess—we're unable to tell whose is whose. The kiss deepens and I melt under her. I've kissed her before, but it was nothing like this. This isn't some show kiss, it's just for us. We don't care how we look or if anyone is watching. This is for our pleasure only.

"I like kissing you," I say as we both stop to catch our breath.

"I like kissing you too." Emily bites down on her bottom lip and I groan.

Her eyes widen and I lean in to bite it instead. My teeth grazing her bottom lip elicits a sharp moan from her lips. I suck on it lightly and she uses the opportunity to slide onto my lap. Her legs hook on either side of my hips, and I can feel her body pressed against mine. Her breathing is labored as I feel her heart race. I grab her ass, grip it tightly in my hands. God, she has so much ass it doesn't even fit in my hands. She rocks her hips lightly against me and I groan in her mouth. I move down to kiss her neck lightly. She moans in my ear, and I shiver in anticipation all the way down to my pussy. I don't know how far this is going, but fuck, I'm going to commit every second of this to my memory. I go back to kissing her, tasting whatever sweet thing she ate on the way over here. I palm her ass. She moves against me, and I'm wet as hell. In all my fantasies, it's never happened this quickly. But I'm not about to complain. Emily licks my lips, and I slap her ass. We're just getting started and she is going to kill me.

TWENTY-ONE

Emily

"**A**re you sure this is okay?" Gus asks, pulling back, and I nod.

"Yes, I definitely am not opposed to any of this." I blush.

That's all the invitation Gus needs, and their mouth is back on mine. Soft lips and hands melt into me. They push hair out of my face and hold one hand on my cheek, the other starting to explore my body. My hands are in their hair, tugging lightly on the ends as they kiss me harder. Fuck, this is definitely not like one of our public kisses. I can tell this is all for me. There is no intention behind this except desire.

Gus grabs my boobs, and my head falls back onto the couch. Even through the thin cotton shirt I'm wearing, my nipples are pebbling under their touch. I want to reach for Gus's chest but I don't know if I should. I know they wear a binder, but we haven't had that talk yet, and the last thing I want to do is make them uncomfortable. Before we move any further, I decide to stop and ask.

"Everything okay?" Gus asks, eyes worried.

"I wanted to check in, maybe ask about certain things. Set any boundaries we might need…"

"That's actually really smart." Gus steadies their breathing and fixes their messy hair.

"I don't really have any boundaries, but I didn't know if certain things were off limits for you…"

"Ah, I don't like my breasts being touched. I usually take off my shirt when I'm comfortable but they're not usually on display. I keep my bra on and ask that you give more attention to the rest of my body," Gus explains.

"Works for me; I just didn't want to like do the wrong thing," I say.

"I appreciate you asking. So you don't have any boundaries you need to set? Does that mean I can have my way with you?" Gus asks, wiggling their eyebrows and laughing.

"Oh yes." I laugh, but I mean it.

I know in the past I thought Gus handled everything with care, but right now they are proving me wrong. With desire in their eyes and the way their hands dig into my skin, I'm a match begging to be lit. I can feel everything as they hold my wrists and pull me toward their bedroom. They stop to pin me against the wall, and I feel their teeth drag against the nape of my neck. They bite down just hard enough to cause an audible moan, and I almost collapse into their touch. Weeks of tension are boiling over into this moment. How many times have I imagined this happening? How many fantasies played in my head as I touched myself?

"Tell me what you like, Pretty Girl." Gus dubs me a new nickname, and I feel my panties sticking to my center.

"I—I, *this*. This, I like." I try to form an actual sentence but their mouth on my neck makes that impossible.

"Come on, babe, a little kissing and you're unable to tell me what you like?" Gus is getting off on this—the fact that I'm barely a person right now.

"I bet you're just as wet as I am." I growl.

"But I'm the one in control," Gus says as they place a tattooed hand around my neck. I whimper as they tilt my head up to look them in the eye. Like a tiger ready to pounce, Gus is ready to take me to bed. I just have to say the word.

"Please, just fuck me," I grumble, conceding easily.

"Thought you'd never ask." Gus places a chaste kiss on my forehead before bending down. They swing me over their shoulder, giving me a view of their perfectly round ass as they carry me into the bedroom.

Gus plops me onto the bed with a sound of resistance from the mattress. They take their time kicking off their pants and socks, leaving them in a T-shirt and a pair of boy shorts. I groan, taking in all of Gus's tattoos. Their legs are covered in ink. I won't have enough time to see everything this second, but the sight of their thick tattooed thighs goes right to my pussy. I kick my legs, shimmying off my pants and socks too, to even the playing field. I didn't know this was going to happen, but I had hopes, so I'm groomed and wearing the right kind of panties.

"Holy hell, Pretty Girl." Gus groans, seeing my pink thong. They run their hand over it and slap the wet spot in the middle.

"Fuck," I whimper out. Sex with Gus is about to be better than anyone before, I can just tell.

"I know exactly where I want you, Pretty Girl," Gus says, bending down to kiss me.

They lean on the bed, their arms holding them up as I slip my tongue around theirs. They taste like nostalgia, like I'm somehow craving and remembering something I've never felt before. Gus groans as I bite down on their bottom lip. Their left hand grips my thigh while the other one pulls me over to crawl on top of them. In one swift movement, I'm somehow straddling Gus's waist. Their hands are in my hair, tightening around the ponytail I'm wearing and pulling me into their mouth. I grind on their lap, my body begging for more friction.

Gus's hands leave my hair so they can take off my T-shirt. It goes over my head in an instant and onto the floor somewhere. I'm in my no-bra era, so my tits plop down and Gus groans. It's only a second before their mouth is all over them, licking and sucking on my nipples. As I grind my hips, I hit my clit against their hips.

"Oh shit." I groan as their lips latch to my breast.

Gus hums against me and I move even faster. I'm barely doing anything, but my clit is hitting just right and I'm wetter than whatever river you can think of. The fabric of my thong bunches at my clit, making the friction even hotter. The more I move, the more turned on I get, and the closer I get to chasing this orgasm. Gus's tongue swirls around my nipple and then over the next. As they keep it going, I can feel myself about to come. Has it really been that long that I'm coming from some grinding and nipple play? I guess so. Gus grips my ass with their hands and moves my hips even faster, and I lose control.

"Yes! Yes! Yes! Oh shit, I'm—" My voice is a muffled mess as my orgasm takes over and I can only see stars. I moan out in pleasure and collapse into Gus.

"God, I thought you singing was my favorite sound. But I might have a new favorite," Gus whispers in my ear. A shiver runs up my spine and I lean in to kiss Gus's neck.

"Since we're just getting started, I have a request," Gus says.

"Okay?"

"Please sit on my face," Gus begs. Something about seeing this tattooed person who is usually in control, beg for me to sit on them makes me wild.

I climb off Gus and undress completely, my soaked thong doing nothing to help anyway. Gus moves back on the bed, laying their head on the pillows. I give them a quick kiss before climbing on top of their face and lowering over them. As I line up with their mouth, Gus grips my thighs, and I rock slowly against them. Their tongue starts immediately running through my slit, slurping up every drop of my wetness. I look down, watching as their eyes struggle to stay open and watch as I play with my breasts. I tug on my nipples, which are now sensitive and covered in light hickeys. Squeezing them and playing with them as I moan and rock my hips. Gus's tongue feels even better on my pussy than it does in my mouth. They suck lightly on my clit, and I grip the headboard so I don't fall over.

"Oh my gosh!" I cry out, and I can feel Gus smiling against me.

I move my hips in a circle and my pussy glides all over Gus's face. I've never been this wet in my life, but this is months in the making. Why the hell did we wait so long to do this? Gus's fingers dig into my thighs and then one hand lets go to slap my ass. Every time I rock my hips forward, Gus rewards me with a slap hard enough to leave a mark on my ass. I can feel the stinging sensation along with the heat from each slap.

"Fuck! Right there!" I cry out and Gus slaps my ass one last time before I come, gripping the headboard. "Gus! Oh Gus!"

I'm screaming but I don't give a shit. I couldn't contain it if I wanted to. The second orgasm rushes over me even harder than the first one. Gus doesn't stop licking me clean until I fall into bed next to them. My pussy is throbbing from all the action. I need a second to catch my breath. God, I'm going to have to pace myself with Gus.

"You look so hot sitting on my face," Gus whispers in my ear. They nibble lightly on my earlobe, and I shudder. My body is like a live wire right now, and I can't contain it.

"You're going to kill me," I grumble.

"Death by orgasms seems like a good way to go," they say in between kisses along my collarbone.

"No, no; it's your turn." I push them off me and slide in between their thighs.

Gus is bigger than me, with more body and squish, so there's not too much space until they spread their thighs. They took their panties off at some point and I admire their glistening pussy. It has a cute little tuft of dark curls, and their wetness is dripping down their thighs.

"Can I?" I look up at Gus, who is patiently waiting for me to touch them.

"Fuck, please." They nod.

I touch the tip of my tongue to their clit and Gus's hips jolt off the bed. I smirk, knowing I have control over them for once. Before they can complain, I press my face into their pussy. Their hand knocks into mine and I intertwine my fingers in theirs. I lap up the taste of them—God they taste so fucking sweet. With every lick, they get wetter, and I just want more. Is it possible to become addicted to the taste of something that isn't food? Gus's hips rock against me and their fingers dig into mine as they wrestle with how slow I'm taking this. I have a feeling if I go faster like they want, they'll be chasing their orgasm in seconds. But I want this to last, so I take my time getting to know their body. Their free hand pushes my head down and pulls my pony-tail tightly around their fist.

"God Em, fuck, please," Gus begs. A sound I will remember for a long, long time.

"Well, if you're going to beg," I say, looking up at them with their wetness dripping off my chin.

"Em, please," they beg again.

This time I listen and suck on their clit. I run my tongue through their folds in a faster motion and Gus's reaction is instant. They pull my hair tightly and a stream of moans and whimpers come out of my sexy partner. Their body shakes and their thighs crush my head like a headband on too tight. I can taste their release, and they don't relax until it fully passes. Knowing I can make Gus come is enough to make me wet all over again. Between the sounds and the taste, I know this is the beginning of a very long night.

TWENTY-TWO

Gus

I'm breathless as Emily lies next to me. I pull her into my chest, and she lays on my breasts, something I don't typically love. But with her it feels safe. I want to feel close to her right now. We pull the sheets over our naked bodies, and she trails her soft fingertips over the outline of my tattoos. She starts on the ones on my arm and goes to my hand then back again. I kiss the top of her head and breathe in her familiar scent. Her stomach growls and we both start laughing.

"It's not my fault! I was promised dinner!" she complains.

"I'm sorry, we can order food. What time is it anyway?" I twist my wrist to look at my watch. It's just after ten fifteen. There are more than a handful of places nearby that are still open.

"Can we still get Thai food?" Emily asks, looking at me with wide, bright blue eyes.

"Yes, what do you want? I'll grab my phone." I get up and look around the room for my pants but then I realize my phone is still in the living room.

"Pad Thai please! But gluten-free!" Emily calls as I find my phone sitting on the coffee table.

I call and place an order. By the time I put my pants and shirt back on, it's here. That's New York City food service for you. Even at night, most restaurants are fast food.

"I'll get dressed—" Emily starts but I cut her off.

"Stay in bed and I'll bring it to you. And definitely don't put on any clothes." I wink.

I stop in the kitchen to get us some water and then head back to the bedroom with the food. She looks comfortable, sitting in my bed with the sheet over her lap. Her breasts are exposed, showing off the chest tattoo I did for her. Blonde hair is pulled back neatly into a fresh ponytail, and her body is flushed from earlier. She is breathtaking. How the hell did I end up with a pop star in my bed?

After we both eat, we end up taking a quick shower together —which becomes more of a cold-water quick rinse after kissing too long led the hot water to run out. As she dries her hair with my hairdryer in the bathroom, I clean up the mess of clothes from earlier and get the bed ready for tonight. She hinted that she might be up for a little more sex before bed, and I definitely want to take advantage of that. I want to explore every inch of her.

Before she comes back, I look in my closet for a box of supplies I haven't used in a while. The strap on is clean and safe. I don't make a habit out of using it with every partner. But I really want to use it with Emily. I love being the one to wear it, and the thought of her on the other end is more than a few fantasies I've imagined. I put it in the nightstand to keep it close; I don't want to pressure her but if she's interested, I won't have to go far.

"I wish I brought more panties. I didn't think mine would get ruined." Emily sighs, walking into the room.

She's naked, her body on full display with no shame. Her ass is round and thick, bouncing with every step. Her full breasts almost do the same, her perky pink nipples firm and taut. Her creamy white skin is soft, blonde hair now dried is hanging down her back. I watch as she saunters toward me. Every inch of her is a dream. I can feel myself getting weak just watching her. How the hell am I supposed to go on now that I know what she looks like naked? I'll have to quit my job and only please her.

"Why are you looking at me like that?" She laughs nervously.

"You're so fucking beautiful," I murmur. Closing the distance between us, I hold her face to look at me. "You are so beautiful, and I'm so lucky."

Emily blushes and I press my lips to hers. Her naked body touches mine and I'm feeling way too overdressed for the occasion. She's smaller than me, but we match in height. Spinning her around, I let her face the mirror. I slide my hand down her front, and she can see everything happening in the mirror.

"Tell me what you want," I whisper in her ear. She closes her eyes as my fingers glaze over her clit.

"I need you to fuck me again," she says quietly.

"How would you feel if I fucked you with a strap on?" I ask. Emily shudders and nods, her body reacting at the thought before she can speak.

I lead her to the bed, and she sits on the edge, waiting for me. I pull off my clothes except the sports bra I'm wearing over my binder. I take the strap out of the drawer and slide it on. Before I fuck her with it, I watch the way her eyes follow it with desire.

"Get on your knees and make it wet," I tell her.

Emily drops to the ground, sits on her knees, and peers up at me. She takes it with her hand, moving it into her mouth, and begins sucking on it. It's erotic as she gives the strap a blow job. Using all her spit, she leaves it dripping wet. So I tell her to get back on the bed, on her knees, and position myself behind her. She's already wet, her pussy dripping in anticipation of what is about to come. I slap her ass hard, watching my handprint appear once again.

"Come on, Pretty Girl, I want to see how bad you want me," I tell her.

"I want it so bad, I'm soaked." She whimpers.

I move the head of the strap to touch her center, teasing her slightly as I move my hips back and forth. Every time I pull away, she moves back, trying to find what she lost. I tease her a few more times until I suddenly fill her up. Gasping, her face falls down into the bed and her ass sticks higher in the air.

"God, you look so good bent over like a slut for me," I tell her.

"Fuck." Emily whimpers.

I'm grateful the nickname wasn't taking it too far, but it seems to fuel her. As I move inside her, she's so wet that the strap keeps falling out. Like she's an overflowing river, I can't seem to stay inside her. She's groaning and complaining every time it falls out. Her body wants more and is only making it harder to stay in. I take it out, rub off some of her juices and slide it back in. Emily moans and I use her hips to steady myself. I pound into her pussy harder and harder as she reaches between her thighs to touch her clit.

"Such a good slut, touching yourself. You must want to come so badly, huh?" I slap her ass harder and harder.

"God yes!" Emily cries out.

"Say my name. Cry it out so everyone knows who makes you scream like a slut, Pretty Girl."

"Fuck! Gus! Please, don't stop, I'm coming! Gus! Gus! Gus!" Emily screams as I slam into her pussy uncontrollably. I slap her ass once more and I don't stop thrusting until her legs go limp and I fall out.

Emily slumps onto the mattress, her face to the side with her ass still in the air. Her pussy is pink and dripping juices down her legs. Getting down on my knees, I start eating her out. I need another taste, and she's laying there showing me. She starts to whimper under me and her thumb brushes across her clit lazily as I lick her from top to hole. Eating ass has never been my thing, so I stay in my lane and her body reacts deeply when I slide my tongue inside her.

"Oh, fucking hell."

I can't talk, but if I could I'd tell her how good she tastes and how I'm going to eat her for every meal. Emily is on the brink of an orgasm, and I pull away at the last second. She cries out in annoyance, and I slide a finger inside her, then another. She touches her clit, and I pump my hand in just for a second as Emily comes again. She's yelling, but her voice is muffled by the sheets so I can't make out what she's saying. She finally rolls over and I lay down next to her.

"It's a good thing you don't always have that, or we'd be doing that all the time," Emily says, eyeing the strap.

"All I heard from that is I should start wearing it under my clothes." I wink.

Emily laughs but it's hoarse, so I grab her glass of water and she takes a sip. I take her hand in mine, and she puts the glass back down. Her thumb rubs the side of my hand softly, as if to reassure me of something. I relax and my eyes start to close. I hate to admit I'm tired but I did work all day.

"Someone needs some sleep." Emily smiles as she catches my eyes fluttering.

"I gotta rest up if I can give you more orgasms tomorrow."

"Mmm, sleepover?" Emily asks lazily.

"Duh, if you think I'm letting you go home tonight, you're crazy."

"Be careful, you sound like some of my fans," Emily teases.

"Some of your fans would go lethal if they knew what we were up to tonight," I say.

"Some would also pay millions." She laughs.

"Too bad this is between us."

"The world couldn't handle it."

"Does this change anything like public-wise? Do you want us to be more private with our relationship?" Emily asks.

"No, I knew what I was getting myself into. I like you and all the things that come with dating a pop star." I smile. "But maybe we keep the multiple orgasms to ourselves," I tease.

"Georgie is going to be so smug about that." She groans.

"What?"

"She's been saying for weeks there was something between us, and I told her it was all in her head. So when I don't come home tonight, she's going to be throwing a party, I can tell." Emily sighs.

"Well, I'm not going to apologize for that."

"Oh, you wait, she'll be unbearable with you too."

"I welcome it."

Emily leans in to kiss me, a lazy kiss that starts off as a peck and leads to more. Her lips are tired, as are mine, but I can taste myself on her. She smiles halfway through and lays her head on the pillow with a yawn. I reach for the lamp, turning off the last of the lights, and plug my phone in next to us.

"Do you have to be up early tomorrow?" Emily asks.

"I have work at one, but I'm more than happy to call out," I admit.

"You don't have to."

"Are you kidding me? Having sex with you all day or going to work? It's a no-brainer. I'll text River right now." I laugh.

I type a quick text, realizing it's after two a.m. But I never use my sick days, it isn't like the place can't function without me.

RIVER: are you calling out at 2 a.m. because the pussy is that good?

ME: Oh my god. Pleading the fifth

RIVER: Aspen and I say get some, enjoy your day off

I start laughing. "What?" Emily asks, so I show her the phone. "Oh my god! So much for keeping that between us." She laughs.

"I guess calling out of work at 2 a.m. is the sign of a good lay," I tease.

TWENTY-THREE

Emily

When I wake in the morning, I forget for a split second where I am. But Gus's tattooed arms are around me, and I relax as I remember last night. The memory of all we did sends a shiver straight to my pussy. God, I knew Gus was amazing, but I lost track of how many orgasms they gave me. They are still fast asleep, so I grab my phone and sneak into the bathroom to go pee. One of their cats, I think Bitsy, sees me in the hallway and rubs against my bare calf. I bend down to pet them and then close the bathroom door behind me. After peeing and washing my hands and my face, I look at my phone to see if I missed anything. It's only eight a.m., so that explains why I still feel tired. I have a handful of texts from Georgie, so I decide to call her.

"Are you okay?!" she asks, anxiously picking up the phone.

"Yeah, I just saw all your texts."

"But it's eight a.m. What are you doing awake?" She sounds suspicious.

"I got up to pee. I'm going back to sleep."

"I take it went well, considering you had a sleepover." She sounds smug; I knew this was coming.

"You *might* have been right about Gus's feelings for me," I admit with a groan.

"I knew it! Damn, I wish I placed actual money on this! I'd be so rich right now!" she cheers.

"Yeah, yeah. Anyway, we had a sleepover and I'll be here again today, so don't worry about me."

"Good, I checked your location before bed and saw you were still there. I assumed it was going well, or I would've called."

"Well, I'm glad you didn't. They gave me at least five orgasms," I whisper.

"Holy shit, doesn't that hurt your vagina?" Georgie asks. Of course it's the straight girl who doesn't understand how amazing multiple orgasms can be.

"No. I mean yeah, I'm sore today but holy shit. Totally worth it."

"Good, go sit on some ice. You can tell me all about it when you're done with your sex adventure. I have to get ready for work." She laughs.

"Okay, love you G."

"Love you too, E."

I head back to Gus and slip back into my spot in their arms. They peek open an eyelid to look at me and then pull me in tightly again. I relax and close my eyes, willing myself to fall back asleep. With a yawn, I'm back asleep in a matter of minutes.

When I wake up again, Gus isn't in bed. It's chillier than it was last night, so I pick up Gus's T-shirt off the floor and slide it on. I head out into the living room and find Gus sitting on the floor next to all three of their cats.

"Good morning." I smile.

"Good morning. Sorry, they wanted breakfast, and I always give them pets after," Gus says.

"No worries." I bend to place a quick kiss on their lips.

"God, you look good in my clothes." Gus groans.

"Probably because it barely covers anything." I laugh. It

barely hangs to the middle of my thighs; one cool breeze and everything will be on display.

"Mm." They bite their bottom lip and wink at me.

"Before that, I need some coffee. Do you have a mug?"

"Uh yeah, it's in that cabinet." Gus points to the top cabinet—the one I have to stand on my toes to reach. As I do, my shirt lifts all the way up to the tops of my hips.

"There aren't any mugs in here!" I say, but as I turn around, I realize they lied to get me to flash them. "Hey! You're so bad!"

Laughing, Gus walks over and grabs me a mug from the lower cabinet. They kiss me softly and I shake my head.

"Sorry, I saw an opportunity."

"Well now you need to make me coffee too," I pout.

"Sounds good, Pretty Girl. Do you want some breakfast?"

"Mmm, maybe eggs?"

"Of course. Have a seat, and I'll take care of everything."

I watch as Gus makes me a cup of coffee first, asking how I like it, and makes everything perfectly. While I drink my coffee, they make a feta and spinach omelet for each of us. It's delicious, and then we both head back to the bedroom.

"We can watch a movie or something if you want," Gus suggests.

"I had a different kind of entertainment in mind," I say, kneeling on the bed.

They turn around to face me, and I throw their T-shirt off and at them. I giggle as Gus climbs on top of me, kissing my neck and behind my ear.

"You're going to be the death of me, Pretty Girl," Gus grumbles, and I moan lightly.

"It's hardly fair when I'm so underdressed," I say, and Gus laughs.

Standing up, they make a show of getting undressed for me. They keep on their sports bra but take everything else off, and I groan. They are a tattooed Greek God. Their body gets me hot, and I can't wait to taste them again. Gus climbs onto the bed and lays me down in the center. They take their time touching and kissing my body, careful not to touch my pussy. I know it is their way of teasing me, and it's working.

Gus tugs on my nipples. "Oh!" I call out.

"God, I can feel how wet you're getting on my thigh." Gus smirks and moves their thigh to hit my clit. I try to grind on them but they still my hips.

"Not yet, Pretty Girl." Gus winks and I whimper.

They go back to touching my breasts, their tongue torturing my nipples as I try to get some friction down lower. Gus takes my hands and holds them above my head so I can't move them. They kiss my chest, down my stomach and back up again, all the way to my neck. Shivers run through my body, and I clench my pussy, desperate to feel something more. Gus keeps playing with my tits and then slides their hand across my pussy.

"Oh!" I cry out, moaning and whimpering as they start to slip two fingers inside me. "Oh, shit!"

"Good?" Gus asks innocently.

"Mmm." I nod furiously, and Gus curves their fingers.

My head falls back into the pillow, and I can't form anything besides a plethora of moans. Gus fingers pump in and out of me while their tongue twists around my nipple. I play with the other one, copying exactly what Gus does to me with their tongue. Their fingers start to move faster, and I feel an orgasm building. But then I feel a different pressure and I panic as I realize what it is.

"Gus! Gus! I'm going to squirt!" I cry, but Gus doesn't stop. Only pausing for a split second before looking up at me with dark eyes. Oh, fuck! They're going to let me. They want me to squirt for them.

Not pulling out their hand, I feel the pressure build until it releases everywhere. I've only squirted a handful of times, and it was mostly on my own. Gus's hand is dripping wetness when they pull it out of me. My thighs are soaked, the sheets under me are soaked, but I'm panting, trying to catch my breath from that release. God, it was like I let everything in me go. It's different than an orgasm but still an intense and beautiful release.

"Fuck, that was so hot," Gus mutters from between my legs. They disappear to grab a towel, but when they come back, they take a warm washcloth and brush it over my pussy. They clean my thighs and everything from my mess.

"I'm so sorry, I ruined your sheets."

"Nah, nothing the wash can't get out." Gus shrugs. "Why don't you sit on the chair, and I'll change them. If you're cold, you can put on my shirt."

Gus hands me a shirt and places a towel on their soft chair in the corner. I didn't notice it before, but it looks comfortable. I put the shirt on before sitting and watch as they carefully clean everything up and bring me a glass of water.

"You okay?" Gus kneels next to me.

"I am, yeah." I smile.

I'd never felt this taken care of before. I never wanted to do that with anyone else before because I didn't know how they'd react to the mess. But Gus is more worried about how I'm feeling than the way their sheets will look tomorrow. I'd hooked up with men before I realized I was a lesbian, and while it was a disappointment for obvious reasons, it definitely never felt like this. Even my other relationships felt more about a quick lay than actually connecting. I feel safe with Gus; I know I can trust them.

"Do you want to watch a movie in bed?" Gus asks.

"What about you? You didn't come." I frown.

"So? You look exhausted and I'm more than satisfied right now." Gus kisses my forehead.

"Okay." I know they're not lying to me. I can feel it in my heart, but I also know that's not the kind of relationship we have. They are always honest with me.

We put on some new rom com, but we aren't really watching it. Gus is playing with my hair and I'm thinking of song lyrics in my head. Something new, something about Gus. Something that truly terrifies me, if I'm being honest. Which is why I don't write the lyrics down. It would be like admitting out loud that they're true, and I'm not ready for that.

The rest of the day, Gus and I take turns asking each other things to get to know each other better. We play with their cats, we order in more food, and we have lots of sex. It's domestic and cute and it might just be the best day I've ever had. I don't know what it is about Gus, but being with them makes me feel like I can handle anything. They kiss my forehead and hold my hand, and I know deep down, they wouldn't care if I wasn't LULY. They want me for me. There's no fear that they're in this for some ulterior motive.

"You're so cute when you're focused on something," Gus murmurs.

"Sorry, I was paying attention." I shift focus back to the movie playing.

"No, you weren't, but that's okay." Gus laughs.

"It is?"

"Sure, if I had to guess, whatever you were thinking about it more important than the end credits of a movie we didn't watch," they say, and I realize I missed the entire movie.

"I was thinking of song lyrics," I admit.

"Anything good?"

"Just a really good breakup song," I say sarcastically. But when Gus doesn't laugh, I realize they think I'm serious. "I'm joking! Sorry I thought you knew that."

"Way to give a guy a heart attack." Gus clutches their chest and lets out a deep breath.

"I'm sorry." I nuzzle my face into the space between their neck and collar bone.

"It's okay." Gus kisses my hair, and I relax under their touch.

I start to hum an unfamiliar melody, and I realize this song was writing itself. I can't recall the last time I wrote a love song that I meant. Most of them are generic or inspired by things, but never have I written one with a person in mind. Is there such a thing as a like song? No, probably not because that sounds sort of shitty. But that's what I needed. At least for now. I don't want to rush into anything and ruin it by going at hyper speed. So I hum lightly and hope I'll remember the lyrics for when I'm ready to sing them.

TWENTY-FOUR

Gus

"Are you ready for this?" Emily asks quietly, sitting next to me in the back of a fancy limousine.

"I think so?" I adjust my tie again to make sure it's straight.

I'm out of my depth, but I'm wearing my fanciest black suit, complete with a pink tie that matches Emily's dress. It took everything in me not to rip it off her once I saw her in it. Her dress is floor length, pink and sparkly, but hangs tightly around her body and is completely backless. Which also means she isn't wearing a bra, and her tits look amazing.

"It's a little intense when we first get out, but once we get inside, it'll be okay," Emily reassures me with a smile and a gentle squeeze of my hand.

"Okay." I nod.

It's our first public appearance since we started officially dating last month. Most of our time has been spent indoors, which cannot be shared with the public. So Viv wasn't thrilled and insisted we choose some events that can showcase our romance. Emily and I chose the LGBTQ+ charity art gala. It's an event hosted inside one of the city's nicest hotels and only the elite were invited. Emily said the buy-in was something like fifty thousand dollars a person. But it all goes to at-risk LGBTQ+ youth right here in the city.

The limousine pulls to a stop and the doors open. Emily gets out first to an array of cheers and excitement. She holds her hand out, and I let out a deep breath before taking it and joining her on the rainbow carpet. That is cute. Paparazzi are taking photos, a security guard in a tux is leading us to the press and where we'll pose for photos. Everyone is shouting Emily's stage name, and I'm trying to keep up.

Emily and I stop, and we pose for a few photos together. Then they ask Emily to be alone, so I take her clutch and stand back so I'm not in the way. Emily captivates the attention of everyone there. Every camera is on her and she effortlessly poses like a model. When she's done, she joins me with a quick peck on the cheek. Heading inside, we stop to answer some questions about our relationship with the press.

Viv appears out of nowhere in a long black dress and a grimace on her face. Does that woman ever smile? She taps her imaginary watch at Emily, who sighs.

"I have to do the interview with Pride11 in five minutes. Do you wanna grab a drink and we can meet at our table?" Emily asks.

"Sure." I nod and she hands me a ticket. "Good luck." I kiss her, and she disappears with Viv.

I walk farther inside the building and find the bar serving drinks. I get a tequila sunrise and look around the room. It's draped in sheer rainbow curtains to make the light inside look like a rainbow. There's a stage and a podium at the front, with a team of people setting up the microphones. Each table is round, with a rainbow number sign in the middle. I find my table and take a seat but there is no one with me so I take a sip of my drink and look around.

I feel a little out of place but I know I'm not here for me. This is the kind of thing Emily needs me to do so she could continue being LULY. And I saw firsthand how happy it makes her to be onstage, so I want to do everything I can to make sure she doesn't lose that.

"Gus?" My name being called makes me twist in my seat. I jump up when I realize it's Kenzie calling my name.

"Holy shit! What are you doing here?" I greet her with a hug.

She's wearing this dazzling black dress that shows off her full figure. Her wife, Barbie, is behind her in a pink dress similar to Emily's but different enough there won't be a report in any magazines.

"I'm a gay supermodel, did you think I wouldn't be here?" She laughs. Of course she's at an event like this.

"Barbie, it's good to see you again." I smile.

"Is your girlfriend here? I heard she was on the guest list," Kenzie asks.

"She's doing an interview right now, but she's here somewhere. I definitely want you to meet her." I smile. Especially now that things were real, I want Kenzie to see that I'm happy with someone.

"We're at table eight, why don't you find her and bring her over? I have a few people to say hello to." Kenzie smiles and I nod.

"Okay, I think I'll get her now."

I go to look for Emily. She's probably done with the interview by now and I don't want her to miss meeting Kenzie. I look around the press room, trying to see if I spot my girl. A flip of blonde hair catches my eye, and I see her across the room. It's right by another set of doors, so I go the long way to get her so I'm not accidentally in the middle of any other media. Last thing we needed was the headline of *LULY'S PARTNER CAUSES MEDIA BLACKOUT AFTER RUINING SEVERAL INTERVIEWS*. When I come around the other side, Emily's back is toward me so she can't see me, but I can hear everything.

"Would you give our fans any insight to your relationship with Gus?" the reporter asks.

"We like to maintain a pretty private life," Emily says.

"Is it a serious relationship?" the reporter questions.

"I'd say it is, yes."

"Are you in love?" The reporter is nosey as hell, but I want to hear her response. This isn't something we've talked about yet.

"I think I'm getting there. Falling in love takes time, and if they're patient, I think I just might be."

"Wow, you heard it here folks. LULY is falling in love. We wish you and Gus all the best, and thank you for joining me tonight."

"Thanks for having me, Jeremiah," Emily says.

The interview ends when someone yells *cut!* And then it's all murmurs. I can't hear anything else they're saying without the microphones. But my heart is beating in my ears anyway. Emily is falling in love with me? Did she really mean that? I knew she had to, because why would she lie about something like that? Emily made a point of telling it like it is, especially when it came to our relationship. Was that why she didn't want me to hear it?

"Oh! Gus!" Emily rounds the corner and almost bumps into me.

"Hey." I kiss her cheek, and she stills.

"You've been here the whole time?" Her eyes widen, and I get confirmation that what she said was real.

"Uh no, I just came to find you. My best friend, Kenzie, and her wife are here so I wanted to introduce you," I say quickly. I hate lying to her but I don't want her to be nervous about what I heard. Or feel any pressure to say something before she feels ready.

"Oh okay, I'd love to." She relaxes and takes my hand, letting me lead her back to the party.

Kenzie and Barbie aren't at the table, but we find them grabbing a drink and I get Emily one too. Barbie and Emily hit it off right away, talking about the other's dress and who designed it. They start talking like they're old friends and I laugh. I'm glad Emily is getting along with my friends so well.

"You two look really good together," Kenzie says.

"Thanks, this is my fanciest suit."

"You know that's not what I meant." Kenzie laughs. "You both look happy together."

"Thank you, I think we are," I say with ease.

"I hate to break up this party, but we have to say hello to a lot more people tonight. I'm fundraising for the event and the more hands I shake, the more we make," Kenzie says interrupting Barbie and Emily exchanging numbers.

"We're going to get tea someday," Emily says smiling at me.

"Sounds amazing."

The event itself is sort of boring. It's mostly rich people talking to other rich people about how rich they are. Emily doesn't know anyone except a few influencers who are too busy documenting everything to say hello. I'm silently grateful Cari isn't one of the influencers here. I don't want to see her again anytime soon. She's texted me a few times to apologize, but I've left them unread. I don't want to look back at my past with her. I'm moving on to my future with Emily.

"Do you wanna get out of here?" Emily whispers halfway through the dinner.

"What? I thought we couldn't leave," I whisper back.

"We can sneak out the side entrance. Go get tacos instead of this food I can't even eat," she whispers seductively. Or maybe it just sounds seductive because it's my girl whispering in my ear about tacos.

I nod, and she stands first, taking my hand. We duck down as we make our way out of the room. If anyone cares, no one says anything. Emily stops to place a check in the donation bin and then leaves with her hand in mine. If I had the money she does, I'd give back too, but I need all the money I have for now. Emily leads us out of the service entrance, and as we're leaving, she sees a lone paparazzi, so she pulls me out of the way to hide. Her body presses against mine, my back on the brick building, and I hold my hands on her bare skin.

The silk of her dress feels like a Godsend as I grip it tightly in my hands. Her mouth is only inches from mine, and I can't resist. I lean in to kiss her, drawing all of her in and eliciting a strong moan from her. I silence her with my tongue, my hands on her ass, holding her still as we wait for the paparazzi to pass. At least that's what I tell myself. In reality, I'm trying to get every last second with her. I don't want to wait to touch her, being tortured all night long with this fabric that leaves nothing to the imagination. Or maybe that's just me because I've committed to memory exactly what's underneath.

I don't care how she displays her body, because once we get home, I know it's mine. She's a good slut in the bedroom, only wanting to please me. So her fans and whoever can see what she lets them see. But I'm the only one allowed to touch. I rake my hands over her breasts and her nipples are already hard for me. I toss her blonde curls over her shoulder, and I see a hickey she failed to cover up.

"I already left my mark on you, I see," I whisper in her ear.

"I wanted everyone to see it and know I'm yours," she whispers back.

Using all the strength I have left not to fuck her right here in this doorway, I grab her hand and pull her toward home. We can order something later; right now I need to get us back to the apartment so I can show her all the ways that affects me. She giggles as she sees how turned on I am, and I smack her ass on the way out the door. I'm sure that would make the papers tomorrow but neither of us care. Let the world see how my girl likes to get her ass slapped with a big smile on her face. Hopefully that's a big enough *fuck you* to Viv.

TWENTY-FIVE

Emily

R ehearsal is a little tense today, but I'm not sure why. It seems like everyone is on edge this week even though nothing seems to have changed. The only people who have some sense of normalcy are Viv, Gus, and Georgie. G is visiting me today since they couldn't make the shows this weekend. She hands me a bottle of water as we finish up for the day. Everyone sort of disperses and I look at her with an eyebrow raised. We do that best friend communication where we don't have to say anything out loud. She's not sure what's going on with anyone either but she's going to look and see if there's a full moon tonight. As she pulls out her phone, one of Viv's assistants walks over.

"Do you think we could go somewhere and talk?" she asks quietly, looking over her shoulder, but no one is there.

"Uh sure." I nod. "I'll be back," I tell Georgie, who just nods.

"Look, there's something I want to run by you, and I don't know how to say it," Viv's assistant says.

"I'm sorry, you have to remind me your name." I feel like an asshole for not knowing, but I know it's better to ask now than later.

"It's Marsha. I'm sorry, I know it's not like Viv ever lets us talk to you." She sighs.

"Marsha, hi. Why don't you come to my dressing room and we can chat in private?" I suggest.

She nods and follows me. I unlock the door and let her in behind me. She takes a seat on the couch and pulls out a yellow envelope. The kind people use to transport paperwork and important documents. It's filled tightly, which makes me nervous, like she was about to serve me with jury duty papers or something like that.

"So, what's going on?" I sit down across from her.

"It's not really my place but I was afraid if this got out and you didn't know, it would be worse for you. But the stage crew is planning a walk out." She sighs.

"What?" My jaw drops. My crew? What the hell happened?

"They haven't been paid in the last thirty days and can't afford to wait any longer." She hands me a thick document with a lot of numbers and names.

"I'm sorry. You're saying the entire staff hasn't been paid?" I want to make sure I'm understanding her correctly.

"Yes." She nods. "Viv hasn't paid them and has placed the blame on you."

"On me?!" I gasp. She knows I know nothing about making sure everyone is taken care of—that's why I hired her. To make sure she is doing all that to keep everything running smoothly.

"I have all the proof in there. I wasn't sure if I should come to you. But it doesn't seem like you knew. I mean, why would you go to a charity dinner where a buy-in is fifty thousand dollars when you haven't paid your staff? It seemed like poor taste. Which is when I realized you didn't know. So I did some digging internally and found out some things."

"What things?" I raise an eyebrow.

"Viv has been taking the money from your royalties, and instead of paying everyone, she's been paying one extra employee."

"Who?"

"A person who doesn't exist. Their name is in the documents, but they don't have an ID photo, and no one can tell me who this person is. I think it's an account connected to Viv that she or someone else has access to."

"Viv is stealing from me?" I exhale sharply. The accusation is enough to send a shiver down my spine. She was someone I trusted with every aspect of my business. How the hell could she do this?

"Yes. I mean, unless you're the person on the other end of that account. Which did occur to me but wouldn't make any sense because then she's stealing from you to give back to you."

"How did you find this all out?"

"I went digging. I'm only an intern, so it wasn't like they gave me security access. But Viv also treats us like we're morons and has us reset her passwords for her. I just looked at what was there and figured it out."

"I really appreciate you bringing this to me. I can't believe no one has been paid." I look through the paperwork she gave me and some of it starts to make sense.

"When people started talking about a walk out, I knew that you had no idea. I don't want your career to suffer because of someone else's mistakes. I didn't know who to go to with this because she's my boss."

"Marsha, you do not have to worry. I promise you I will take care of this, and no one will be punished except Viv. And I hope whenever you finish your internship here, you'd consider taking a job as my personal assistant. You're exactly the kind of person I'd want on my team looking out for everyone," I say with a smile.

Marsha's face lights up. "You mean that?"

"Of course. And if that's not the position you're looking for, we can chat about it and find you something here. Standing up to your boss isn't easy but this is necessary. I don't tolerate stealing or lying, and I'm so disappointed that my team hasn't been paid for their hard work." I sigh.

"Thank you. You're honestly not like most of the stars I've met."

"I'll take that as a compliment." I wink.

Marsha stands to go but I call after her.

"There's one more thing you can do for me, I want access to everyone's accounts for direct deposit. I'll stop by the bank, and I plan to pay everyone's missing funds today. They shouldn't have to wait for legal to figure this out and pay everyone back."

"I-I don't know if I can get that. But I know someone who can."

"Okay, don't talk to anyone about this, but get me that list as soon as you can. And if you see Viv, please let her know I'm looking for her," I say.

"Of course." She nods nervously and disappears.

I can't believe Viv. I knew she was a shark. Someone who took no one's crap and fought me on the things I didn't like. But I thought she was rooting for me. I thought we were on the same team. I don't know how she could possibly smile to my face like nothing was wrong and then steal from me and all the hard-working people here. She's messing with people's jobs and livelihoods. I wanted to say Marsha is lying, that all of this isn't true. But as I look over the paperwork, it's clear. There is no way she could've forged anything like this. I check it against the records of my own bank account and the numbers are all wrong. Viv was skimming off the top and not paying anyone. And I didn't notice because it was all going to my savings. I'm so pissed, I swear I'm seeing red. I try to do some deep breathing to calm myself down because I'm too angry right now.

"Emily? You paged?" Viv pops her head in, barely looking up from her phone.

"Please have a seat." I force a smile. Taking out my own phone, I text security to wait outside my dressing room door for my signal. If anything gets out of hand, I want them to be there to help.

"What's going on? I haven't been able to contact my assistants today and I've got a lot of things to do," Viv says with a tired sigh.

"Please put the phone down, this is important," I say as calmly as I can.

"What?" She rolls her eyes but puts the phone down on the table, and I try to figure out where to begin.

"Unfortunately, we're on the midst of a walkout with our crew because apparently they haven't been paid in the last thirty days." I cross my hands over my lap.

Viv's face pales but she quickly composes herself. "Well, there must be some kind of a mix up in billing. I can make a phone call right now and see what's—"

"See, I thought maybe that was true. But then I had a closer look at the paperwork, and it seems like the money was coming out of my account this whole time."

"That's odd, maybe it's just stuck in the system. I've heard that can happen some—"

"I thought that too, but then I checked, and apparently there are only two employees we were paying for the last month. You and a person I've never met nor heard of. Which is suspicious since they're making more than double your salary. You'd think I'd have at least heard of this person." I look at Viv, waiting to see what lie she might try to sell me.

"Maybe it was someone on the hiring end? They made a fake account to try and steal it?" Her voice is low, and I don't think she even believes the lies she's telling.

"I looked into that, too. Now tell me Viv, why wouldn't the staff be getting paid if the money was leaving my account? And why is the money going into your pocket?" I narrow my eyes at her.

"I-I don't know what you're talking about."

"I think you do, and I don't think you thought of a good enough lie in the off-chance you'd get caught."

"So fine, I'll give the money back." She rolls her eyes. Is she really admitting that she took the money?

"That's not the point. It makes me look negligent, and people depend on that money to go into their accounts. You can't take money out of their pockets to fill your own. You're fired."

She smiles, then starts maniacally laughing. "You can't fire me."

"Excuse me?" I raise an eyebrow.

"Your relationship is built on a lie that I orchestrated. You can't fire me without me going to the press with proof of your fake relationship." She smirks.

"You signed an NDA. You're the one who gave me the one to give to Gus," I say, searching for something to get her out of my life.

"I didn't sign anything. I gave it to you and Gus—you're the only two mentioned in that contract. I can do or say whatever I want to the highest bidder." She picks up her phone. "Let's see, TMZ is always promising, or maybe I offer up a spot to the highest bidder. A tell all with pop sensation LULY's ex-manager."

I'm at a loss for words. How the hell can she do this? I know she's a bit of an asshole, but I didn't think she'd turn around and do this to me. It isn't like I wasn't paying her an arm and a leg, but I guess enough was never enough for some people.

"Are we done then?" She picks up her phone and starts for the door.

"I don't want you working for me anymore," I snarl.

"We can't always get what we want, now can we?" She shrugs and saunters out the door.

In a rage, I pick up the nearest item—a mug with my face on it—and toss it at the door. It smashes into a million pieces, and I only feel a little bit better. Dropping to my knees, I feel every emotion at once. Tears cascade down my cheeks, and I have to control my breathing. I can feel the anger taking over, and I don't want to let her win. There has to be another way out of this. I'm not just about to let someone like that continue working for me. But all I feel is the betrayal radiating through my bones.

TWENTY-SIX

Gus

"She asked me not to call you, but she won't leave the room, and I didn't know what to do," Georgie says as I get to Emily's rehearsal studio.

"Did she say what was wrong?" I ask, concerned. I raced over in the middle of my day to make sure everything was all right. I'm out of breath from all the damn stairs on the subway. It's arguably quicker than taking an Uber this time of day.

"No. She was talking to one of the interns earlier but then no one's seen her since." Georgie sighs.

"Okay, I'll see what I can do." I smile at Georgie, and she nods.

"I can't let you in here," security says as I try to walk toward Emily's door.

"Can you at least knock and let her know who's here?" I look up at him. He's huge and towers over me, but I have the delusion I can take him if I need to.

"No. I've been told to stay here and not let anyone in," he says sharply.

"EMILY! I'M HERE! IT'S ME, GUS! PLEASE LET ME IN!" I shout loudly, cupping my hands over my mouth to make it louder. Then I listen but there's no sound, so I try again.

"EMILY! IT'S ME AND I'M GOING TO STAY HERE ALL NIGHT SO YOU MIGHT AS WELL LET ME IN!" I shout again, and I mean it too. I don't have anywhere to be but here.

"EMILY, I SWEAR I'LL KNOCK THIS DOOR DOWN. I'LL GET HURT BUT I'LL TRY IT." The guard cracks a smile at my shouting but doesn't budge.

"Just get in here." Emily opens the door and pulls me in.

The sound of broken glass startles me as I walk in the room. Looking down, I see the remains of something ceramic under my feet. I can't quite make out what it is.

"It's a mug. I was pissed and it was the closest thing to me." Emily sighs and slumps back onto the couch, draping a fuzzy blanket over her.

"What's going on? Georgie called me in a frenzy." I sit at her feet and look at her patiently.

"She shouldn't have; it's not a big deal." But she sniffles, as if proving the opposite of her point.

"Babe, you're crying, and you have security out there. I was ready to take him, but I'm glad you let me go easy on him," I joke, and she cracks a smile.

"It's so stupid, I should've seen it coming. But I didn't and now I'm blindsided and trapped, and I don't know what to do." She sobs.

"Whoa okay, I'm trying to keep up but what's going on?"

Emily takes a large, deep breath before explaining everything to me. Viv has been stealing from her, lying to everyone, and the entire staff hasn't been paid in a month. One of her interns came to her with an envelope of proof, and when she tried to fire Viv, she threatened to do a tell all.

"I don't know what to do. She knows so much, I can't even think about all the things she knows. She could ruin me."

"Hey, okay we're not going to let that happen."

"We?" She looks up at me with raccoon eyes. Her mascara is a mess under her eyes from all the crying.

"Of course. I told you this is for real, and that means sticking around even when it's not so good. So let's figure out the best plan and tackle it together." I reach for her hand and bring it to my lips.

"Okay," she finally agrees.

"Let's bring Georgie in here first, because she's just as worried. I'm sure she'll know what to do," I suggest.

"Okay." She nods.

We let Georgie in, fill her in on everything, and when she's all caught up, she's just as pissed as I am. Georgie and I have been saying what a bitch Viv is for a while, but we didn't have any proof. We thought it was in our heads when we should've listened to our guts. I wish we could've seen this coming and stopped it before it hurt Emily. That's our girl—sure in different ways, but Emily was everything to us.

"Didn't she sign an NDA?" Georgie finally asks.

"No, only Gus did," Emily says.

"Not when you started the relationship. I mean when you signed her on to be your agent. Wasn't there so much paperwork that you had to see a lawyer to make sure it was all standard?" Georgie asks.

"Oh shit, yeah I did."

"Well, do you have a copy of any of that?" Georgie asks.

"Uh, yes! At the apartment. The lawyer said to keep a physical copy of everything in case there was any issues." Emily lights up.

"Okay, then let's head home and look at the paperwork and brainstorm," I suggest.

"Yes, okay." Emily hops up. Georgie and I exchange a look before turning back to Emily.

"We don't want to kick you when you're down, but you have to change your makeup. The press doesn't need to speculate on your raccoon eye makeup," I say as kindly as I can.

"What?" Emily rushes to the mirror. "Oh my God! How did you both not laugh the moment you saw me?!" Emily giggles.

"It didn't seem like the right time." Georgie smiles.

We head back to their apartment and Emily runs to look for the paperwork. Georgie and I settle in the living room with the takeout we grabbed on the way in. We're all sitting on the floor in the living room around the coffee table. It's the biggest table they have where we can spread out all the paperwork easily. Georgie makes margaritas, because it seems like that kind of a night, and I take mine with extra salt on the brim. Which of course makes it difficult to be serious when Emily is trying to talk about the paperwork.

"You need to put your tongue away! I can't focus." Emily narrows her eyes at me, and I stop.

"Gross," Georgie mumbles.

"Okay, this says she's allowed to talk about anything if she's fired." Emily sighs.

"I guess that was put in there so she could write her tell-all book one day," Georgie snarks.

"Wait, but this says in the case of being let go due to poor job performance or illegal activities, each party is allowed to dissolve the contract and the NDA remains intact," Emily says.

"Holy shit, so if you have proof of her literally stealing thousands of dollars and committing fraud, wouldn't that be the illegal activity?" I ask.

"Yes!" Georgie shouts.

"But how are you going to have her let go? Does she have a boss?" I ask.

"She technically works for an agency, but I believe it's all her family. No way would they side with me. But, I have enough here that if I went to the police, she'd be let go because her bad image would reflect poorly on mine. They'd have no choice but to dissolve everything." Emily's face lights up as she realizes this.

"Let me call my cousin and confirm this, but if so, we're going to the police station tonight," Georgie says, pulling out her phone.

"Didn't she just have a baby? It's like one a.m.," Emily says.

"So? She's not sleeping anyway." Georgie waves us off as she dials. "Luna!"

"Thank you for tonight. I know this is a lot, but it means everything that you didn't go when things got tough," Emily says, holding my hand.

"It might take some time, and I'm sure this doesn't help. But I'm going to show you I'm not someone who leaves when the going gets tough. I can weather any storm." I lean forward to kiss her softly.

But a peck quickly turns into more as she slides her tongue in my mouth. I moan quietly as I taste the margaritas on her lips. Her mouth is cold from all the ice and I'm warming her up. Emily scoots closer to me and I reach to hold her face. Her cheek is warm, probably overheating from the alcohol, and our teeth clunk together as she starts to giggle mid-kiss. We try again, her smile prematurely ending the kiss.

"Ew, get a room." Georgie comes back in the room and Emily flips her off.

"So my cousin said we're right and the best thing to do is head to the police station and file a report before Viv has the chance to do anymore damage. The proof the intern gave us should be enough, but you should bring your paperwork too. If all goes well, she could be arrested tomorrow since it's so much money and her job makes her a flight risk," Georgie explains.

We're all elated from the relief of the good news. Since we only had one margarita each, we're not too drunk to go now—so we head out in hopes of good news.

It's almost morning when we get back from the station but at least Georgie's cousin was right. There was enough evidence to get Viv and put her away. I can see how relieved Emily looks, and I know she'll be stronger because of it.

"Can you come to bed?" Emily asks as we get back to her place.

Georgie is already in her room by the time we get in. She's too tired to stay up and attempt to celebrate with us. Not that we are any better. But Emily wants me to sleepover and I won't turn down the chance to hold my girl in my arms. Especially after the day from hell she had.

"Of course." I nod.

We get undressed and the second her head hits the pillow, she's fast asleep. For a moment, I think she's messing with me. When I get a closer look and she's still fast asleep, I know she's serious. I pull her phone from her jeans, putting it on the charger. I grab a makeup wipe from her bedside table and wipe her makeup off. Then I pull the covers over her and climb in next to her. I don't blame her for being off routine tonight, but I'll do anything I can do to make the morning a little bit easier. I have to go to work in the afternoon, but at least I don't have to get up early. Which is be way too soon anyway.

For a little while, I just watch her sleep. She's facing me with her mouth slightly open, only the sound of breathing fills the room. Sure, there's New York City traffic and sounds outside going on too, but I tune all of that out. The only thing I hear is her. Her chest moves lightly with each breath, and I trace the outline of her face with my thumb. One ear is slightly smaller than the other, but it's not something anyone would normally notice. Her blonde hair is in disarray, half of it falling out of the messy bun she had it in today. She's still so gorgeous that it's times like this I have to pinch myself to remember she's mine. When I finally start to get tired, I pull her into my body and wrap an arm around her.

I shut off the last of the lights, check my phone, and put it on the charger, too. River and Aspen stopped by after work to make sure the cats were fed, so I know they're okay. But that doesn't stop me from looking on the Ring camera inside the apartment just to make sure. All three of them are sleeping in different places on my couch. I've noticed that they like to sleep next to each other when I'm not home. Like being together makes them feel more relaxed. I guess people are like that, too. Often going for whoever feels the safest when things are different.

TWENTY-SEVEN

Emily

"How the hell is it already Halloween?" Gus asks as I look through the Halloween costume ideas on Pinterest.

"Well, it's not until next month but I want to be prepared." I shrug. "We have to look cute for River and Aspen's Halloween party."

"Yeah…" Gus doesn't hide their lack of enthusiasm well.

"What?" I put down my phone to give them my full attention.

"I just don't know if I want to go." They sigh.

"Because of Cari?" I guess. It is an unspoken topic between us. Neither of us have heard from Cari since the night of my show. Yeah, she'd texted Gus a few times, but beyond that it's had silent.

"Yeah. River still doesn't know anything, and I just feel awkward." Gus frowns.

"I understand and we don't have to go. But I don't think you should avoid things just because of one person. And if they're stupid enough to try anything, I'll be there to protect you."

"Oh, yeah? You ready to spar this time, Rocky?" Gus chuckles.

"Maybe that's what we should be for Halloween," I joke.

"You should be something sexy."

"I'm always sexy," I argue.

"That's true." Gus kisses my forehead and goes back to cooking lunch in the kitchen.

That is one of the nice things about Gus, they don't want me to change. They know I love showing off my body and they fully embrace it. Never once have they asked me to cover up or stop flashing my fans. They knew I love my body, and I liked to share it. I have always feared when I started seeing someone seriously that they might take issue with that. But to know they actually encourage and embrace my sexuality? Well, that's even hotter.

"I wanna be a sexy bunny. Like from *Mean Girls*."

"What can I be? A normal bunny?" Gus laughs.

"Oh my god, what if you go as a *not-sexy* bunny—like when Monica got Chandler that rabbit costume."

"I love this idea." Gus laughs. I know it's perfect because then we'll both feel comfortable in what we were wearing.

I start googling where to order costumes nearby and place my order right away. I'm late in picking my costume and I don't want there to be any problems.

"I have to get going, but you'll be here when I get back?" Gus asks as they put a plate in front of me. It's gluten-free pasta with grilled chicken and lots of veggies.

"Yes, I'm going to be writing and working on songs. So if I don't text back, that's why," I explain.

"No worries, I hope you have an inspirational day."

Gus stops by to pull my face to theirs and kisses me slow. I want to beg them to stay home and spend more time with me instead, but I know I can't. Gus loves their job, and I don't want them losing the time off in case they really need it. I'm spending the day at their apartment, as I do a lot of the time when they work. I hang out in their bed, play with the cats, sing songs, or binge watch something on TV. Then when Gus gets home from work, we talk about our days, eat dinner together, and have lots of sex all over the apartment. It's a routine that I like.

The drama with my ex-manager has settled, and I don't want there to be any more surprises for now. The police have actually handled something right for once. Yes, I'm shocked, because despite the fact that doing their job is the bare minimum, they often don't meet that requirement. But Viv was arrested, the staff didn't walk out, and I made sure everyone got their money. I personally paid everyone for the thirty days of work plus a generous bonus for staying on and being patient. I encouraged everyone to talk to me if anything like that ever happens again. I'm going to have to wait to get that money back after all the legal proceedings with Viv, but I know it is worth it. I can't let everyone suffer at the hands of one woman's mistake.

Marsha became my personal assistant, which is a lot like Viv's old job. Except everything is run through me, and I thrive on making everyone feel like it's a family. There is a lot less turnover, and everyone seems happier. I know I feel more relaxed when I go to work.

I don't need to get any writing done today, but I do have a surprise for Gus. I've had this in the works for a bit, but I want it to be perfect. It finally feels like the time, and I know I need time to get everything together. I recorded Gus's favorite song, "Love-fool" by The Cardigans onto an album. I'm going to play it for them when they get home and I'll finally tell them I love them. We've both been dancing around the words for a while now, neither of us wanting to rush things or be the first to say it. But then the idea came to me. Singing it will be so much easier for me.

I figure tying it all together with a sexy outfit and a home-cooked meal will be the perfect way to say it. Georgie texted me a preemptive good luck text, but I'm still nervous. I'm pretty sure Gus will say it back, but what if they don't? What if they realize they don't want to be with me anymore? I ignore the intrusive thoughts in my head and relax. I know my partner. Gus is as obsessed with me as I am with them.

"Gus is going to say it back, right?" I ask Gus's cat, Cat Burglar. But of course, he meows and runs away. That seems like a great sign.

I set up the apartment with small candles. I thought about rose petals, but I don't want Gus thinking it's a proposal. I take an extra-long shower, cleaning and shaving every inch of my body. Then I start getting dinner ready while I wear one of Gus's T-shirts. It smells like them and always puts me in a good mood. I'm making gluten-free tacos and nachos, to commemorate one of our first dates. It was then that I realized this thing between Gus and me might be something real. It took me a lot longer to get my head out of my ass after that. Gus is the sentimental type, and I know they'll appreciate it.

They only have a short day at work, so when I check the clock and see they'll be home soon, I start to panic. I quickly change into some lingerie, covering it with a silk robe I keep here. I even put on a pair of pink heels for good measure. I know how much Gus loves fucking me when I'm wearing heels that make me taller than them. As I hear the key unlocking the door, Gus walks in as I light the last of the candles.

"Welcome home, baby." I walk over and put my arms around their neck.

Gus's jaw drops when they see me, and I smile. I've never grown tired of the attention they shower on me. I love how much they appreciate every part of me.

"Is this an anniversary I don't know about?" They raise an eyebrow as I shut the door behind them.

"I thought we could just relax, listen to some music, maybe have dinner?" I suggest.

"Sounds good to me." Gus stops to kiss me. Their kisses trail down my neck, their hands on my breasts, but I pull back knowing if this continues, I'll lose my nerve.

"Hold on, I want the music." I turn on the record player and the song starts to play.

"Ah, you know this is my favorite." Gus smiles.

But as the lyrics start, they realize it's not the Cardigans singing, it's me. I wince, afraid to look at their reaction but when I do, I'm relieved. Gus is smiling, holding their chest with one hand and wiping away a tear with the other. The song continues playing and I walk over to them, and we start to dance slowly. When the song ends, I look up at Gus and I'm suddenly not afraid anymore. I'm not worried about their response at all; I just want them to know how I feel.

"I love you, Gus."

"I love you too, Emily." Gus smiles before kissing me.

The music stops— it's such a short song—and Gus looks at me.

"It's just the one song, so it stopped."

"Can we listen again?" Gus asks.

"Of course." I nod.

This time I sing along quietly, and Gus holds me close to them. We dance around the room as the song plays over and over. I usually hate hearing my voice play back to me, but it's worth it to see Gus like this. We eat a few bites of dinner before Gus carries me to the bedroom. Their hands on my body, their lips on mine, I can feel everything.

"I love you so much." I whimper as Gus brushes their fingers against my skin.

Gus lays me down on the bed and spreads my thighs apart. Before falling to their knees, Gus undresses and takes off everything. Even the sports bra, that they typically leave on. I'm shocked, it's not like I haven't seen Gus completely naked before. We shower together all the time, change in front of each other and sleep naked a lot of the time. But they preferred to keep it on during sex and I've always respected that. It makes them feel more comfortable and more like themself. So taking it off isn't a small move that's lost on me. I know it was another way of Gus letting me in. Baring themself to me in a similar way that I did tonight.

Gus kneels on the ground. I hear a small rip of lace before their tongue twitches against my clit. They flick over my sensitive spot, and I'm instantly moaning for them. Gus knows all the ways to tease me and get me off in a matter of moments. They drag their tongue down the depths of my pussy, and I pull on their hair. They slide two fingers inside me, and I gasp. Gus hooks their fingers inside of me, pumping in and out.

"Fuck yes!" I cry out, and as my release builds, I let go of everything else.

Which is how I end up squirting on Gus's face. With no warning at all, I feel my release but I'm breathless before I can say anything. My wetness shoots all over Gus, and they lap up every drop. They don't give me a chance to apologize before they're trying to make it happen again. I didn't know it was possible, but Gus pushes all the right buttons, and this time they keep their mouth open. As they try to taste all of me, I struggle to keep my eyes open. I want to see how Gus looks as they taste me, but it's too powerful. My orgasm rips through me next, and my legs clamp around Gus's head. My heels perch over Gus's shoulders as I ride their face to oblivion.

"God, I fucking love you." I let loose a string of moans.

Gus looks up at me, panting, their face shiny with my wetness. Their hair is a rumpled mess, and a goofy grin is on their face. God, I know I'm lucky. But I must have some pretty good karma to be *this* kind of lucky.

"I love you, Pretty Girl," Gus says as they wipe off their mouth with the back of their arm. Something about this feels so primal and needy. Before they can attempt to try again, I pull them in for a kiss.

Epilogue

EMILY

I take a final breath before I run onto the stage. Having my lesbian idols and icons of the Gay Word introduce me was a dream. But actually singing on stage at Coachella was unreal. Everyone is screaming my name, and the second I'm on stage they start screaming louder than I've ever heard. The sun is beating down stronger than I'm used to in New York but I'm embracing it. My ass is basically hanging out in the pink shorts I'm wearing and I have easy access to flash my titties to my fans if I want to. Of course my crop top tee is less than classy with the words, 'Save the planet, destroy my pussy' on it.

"WHO'S FUCKING READY COACHELLA!?" I scream into my bedazzled mic and the crowd goes even crazier.

I spent the better part of last year getting more popular. Gus and I'd relationship going viral only made me and my platform more accessible. And once I got rid of Viv and her lying ass, it's been smooth sailing. This is one of the first times Gus and I have even been out in public for a bit. They prefer to live a more behind the scenes vibe and these days when I'm not on stage, I'm usually curled up with Gus. Their apartment became our apartment and while I haven't officially moved out of my apartment with Georgie, I do spend most of my nights there.

I'm belting out the lyrics to one of my pop songs, we all agree it's a great opener. But my mind is on Gus, I can see them dancing and singing along with Georgie in the front row. They insisted on seeing the show from the pit, there's enough security so I'm not worried. They both have been like proud parents for me, cheering me on since the moment I got the call.

I segue into the next song which is a cover of Lovefool by the Cardigans. It took a bit of convincing for that one, but I'd been dying to play it live and there was no better stage. Decked out with literal pairs of scissors behind me, three full screens showing off my every move, I wanted to sing a love song to Gus. The crowd sings along, even the ones who don't really know it are dancing along.

Gus insisted on wearing a t-shirt with my face on it, on the back the words 'sorry, I don't share'. Which made me fall over with laughter the first time she showed me. But now it was an item heavily requested on my merch site. I loved how much Gus loved me and let me be myself but was also so possessive. They admittedly shared a lot of me with the public as it was.

As soon as the song is over, I put my mic on the stand and dance with my backup dancers. Who have become my regulars instead of a few getting fired every week. I shake my ass in a line with them, my back turned to the audience, then I turn around and lift my shirt so they can see my tits. The crowd goes insane but my eyes are only on Gus.

I once asked them if it bothered them that I like showing off my body, especially my tits like this. The only thing they said was, "I'd only have a problem if you let someone else touch them. It's your body and I just hope you'll keep choosing to let me be the only one to touch them.". They understood this wasn't some cry for help or looking to be accepted. I was looking for attention and I got it, I wasn't searching for validation. Plus, I've noticed at the shows where I do show my body, Gus is practically feral for me by the time we're alone. Something I was hoping would be true of tonight.

Georgie was going out with a guy we met last night which I hoped would be aa good change from her luck with New York guys. This one actually asked for her phone number instead of her snap chat like a frat boy. Which meant Gus and I would be at the AirBnb all alone for a few hours. Hours I'd be taking full advantage of. I was exhausted from this trip and I needed a few hours of unwinding and coming with the love of my life.

"I have one last song, this one's for all the lovers! My beautiful partner is in the crowd tonight, can everyone give them a good cheer!?" I shout and Gus turns bright red. They have no idea what I'm about to do, but I knew this is where I wanted to. "Can we get them to come on up here?"

Security, who does know about this plan, carefully helps Gus onto the stage. They bashfully wave to the crowd who goes crazy just seeing them come up here. Georgie is recording, knowing exactly what's going on.

"Gus and I have only been together a bit over a year, but damn what a year that has been. I mean I'M AT FUCKING COACHELLA BABY!" I pull Gus in for a lingering kiss and we get a variety of whistles. "I couldn't have gotten here without them, they are truly the light when things get dark."

One of my dancers runs over, hands me a small pink box and the crowd freaks out. Gus gasps and I drop to one knee.

"I couldn't be here without you and I never want to spend another moment without you by my side. Will you do me the honor of marrying me, Gus?" I pop open the box and show a thin shiny black band. I knew Gus wouldn't want some flashy engagement ring like I did, so I found something that suited them.

"Yes!" Gus nods and I jump up, forgetting about the ring fand throwing my arms around Gus' neck. Our kiss deepens, me momentarily forgetting there's a crowd of people waiting for me to sing again. But I put the ring on Gus, and smile.

"How about one more song?!" I shout to the crowd.

Gus is led to the side of the stage so they won't be in the way and I can't wait for this song to be over. Gus was mine, officially going to be mine for the rest of our lives. I was over the moon with emotion. My singing never felt this good. I take peeks at Gus as I sing, the way they look at me burning into my brain for later.

BONUS Epilogue

1 YEAR LATER...

EMILY

"Are you sure you want to do this?" Georgie asks as she adjusts my veil.

"You're kidding right?" I laugh, I was due to walk down the aisle any second. It wasn't like I was going to suddenly change my mind.

"I have to check! I know there was zero chance you'd say yes but it's my job as maid of honor to ask and have a getaway car ready." She laughs.

"Do you have one?" My eyes widen.

"Well, no. Because I knew you'd say no." We both crack up.

"You seriously are the prettiest bride." Georgie smiles and I can see a tear in the corner her eyes.

"Don't hog the bride! It's time!" My wedding planner and savor, Briar. I spent tons of money to make sure everything was perfect and I would spend a million more to thank her, because so far everything was perfect.

"I need you and River walking down the aisle." Briar ushers Georgie away and I take a deep breath.

Gus and I wanted a smaller wedding, so we secretly eloped a

month ago. Just Georgie, River, a few others and an officiant at a local dance studio. We turned it into a wedding reception for the day and it was magical. Briar had arranged the entire thing, down to the dress I wore. It was entirely us down to my short, off the shoulder wedding dress and the bedazzled tiara on my head. Fresh tattoos on my thigh on display, curtosey of Gus and sparkly heels making me the same height as Gus.

We knew we'd need to do something for my fans or they'd be forever invading our personal moments. So that was today, with tons of acquaintances, celebrities I knew and Gus' extended friends and clients. It had worked in our favor, having something big planned for months gave us our small, intimate wedding. So here I was in a long, white dress with a slit up my thigh and an all pink bouquet. An extra long veil and a pair of pink sneakers hidden under my dress. It was mostly for show, I hated lying to my fans but since Coachella and my growing popularity things had gotten a little intense.

"Gus is at the end of the aisle, the music is about to start and then it's all you." Briar says quietly as she fluffs up the train of my dress.

I can't see anything under my veil, when the doors open, I look down to make sure I don't fall on my face. With all the paparazzi and celebrities here tonight the last thing I needed was to make a scene. As I reach the end of the aisle, a hand reaches for me and I know it's Gus. I can feel it in my bones and everything feels calmer. Like their presence alone is enough to make me feel safe. They raise the veil over my head and I smile.

Their hair is freshly cut, styled and slicked back with gel. Their tattoos are mostly covered by the back suit they're wearing but they look sexy as hell. Tonight we get to go on our honeymoon and I was counting down the hours. Not like we waited for our wedding or anything, we just haven't been able to keep our hands off each other since we got engaged. As soon as I saw that ring on their finger it was like it awoke something primal in me. And the same thing happened as soon as Gus proposed back to me a few weeks later. The officiant is talking but all my focus is on Gus and how good they look.

"Pay attention." They whisper quietly to me and I smile.

"If we can have the rings?"

Gus and I opted to skip the vows for this ceremony. They weren't big on public speaking so I wouldn't put them through that for a crowd as big as this one. It was simple, exchanging of the rings, the I do's and we'd be on the dance floor shaking our asses. Well, me more than Gus but they were occasionally known to bust a move or two.

"You may now kiss the bride." The officiant steps out of the way and Gus pulls me in for a life changing kiss.

I knew I was already their wife, but to be able to publicly share it? I felt like I was buzzing with excitement. Gus' lips melt into mine as they dip me backward and I drop the bouquet. My arms wrapping around Gus' neck and I can hear the cheers and whistling from the crowd. They stand me up, feeling a little dizzy from the kiss, I hold on tightly to Gus as we walk back down the aisle. We were supposed to head right to the reception, but as Gus leads me a different way I don't hesitate.

"Did you need a minute?" I ask, thinking the crowd was too much for them.

"Yes, but only to do this." Gus pushes me gently against the wall, sliding a hand up the slit in my dress. Her palm cupping my core through my lace panties.

"Fuck," I guess Gus was as turned on as I was about being married.

"I want to fuck my wife before we spend the next few hours smiling and dancing. I want to know you're dripping down your thighs for me." Gus whispers in my ear. They blow gently and a shiver runs down my spine.

"Holy hell." I gasp as Gus moves my panties to the side and drops to their knees.

Their tongue connects with my pussy and I'm bucking at the hips. I want to grab their hair and tug on it tightly but I know I can't. We're already going to raise questions, let us not look like we fucked. Gus sucks on my clit as they slide two fingers inside me and I call out their name. So much for not letting everyone know what we're doing. My nipples are hard against the soft wedding dress fabric and every nerve feels like it's on fire.

"Baby, please. I don't think I'm going to last." I admit. The idea of getting caught, people hearing plus the fact that Gus was on their knees in that suit? It was enough to make me cum but the way they moved their tongue had me coming undone.

Gus hums against my pussy and curls their fingers knowing exactly how I like it. They could have me undone in minutes and they were proud of that too.

"Um, Emily? Gus? The photographer wants to take some photos." Briar calls through the door. She was brave to say anything.

I open my mouth to say okay, but of course Gus sucks even harder so instead the words, "I'm coming!" Falls off my tongue. Briar awkwardly shuffles away and I know I need to pay that woman a hefty tip. But right now I'm seeing stars and I really don't care about anything else.

"Fuck, I love the way my wife tastes." Gus wipes their mouth on the back of a napkin and stands.

I catch my breath, fixing my panties and they smirk. They had a habit of calling me 'my wife' when it came to everything. They were addicted to saying it as much as I was to hearing it.

"We owe Briar a lot of money now you know." I scold my partner while I fix the veil that almost fell off my head.

"Worth every penny." Gus kisses my lips and I shiver tasting myself on them.

"Let's go. I will have to return the favor later."

"Good, we have nothing but time Pretty Girl." Gus winks as they open the door for me.

Curious about Isla and Rae's romance?
Check out Bad at Love! Available for Preorder Now!

Also by Shannon OConnor

SEASONS OF SEASIDE SERIES

(each book can be read as a standalone)

Only for the Summer

Only for Convenience

Only for the Holidays

Only to Save You

Seasons of Seaside: The Complete Collection

LIGHTHOUSE LOVERS

(each book can be read as a standalone)

Tour of Love

Hate to Love You

To Be Loved

Inn Love

Love, Unexpected

ETERNAL PORT VALLEY SERIES

Unexpected Departure

Unexpected Beginnings & Endings

Unexpected Days

Eternal Port Valley: The Complete Collection

STANDALONES

Electric Love

Butterflies in Paris

All's Fair in Love & Vegas

Fumbling into You

Doll Face

Poolside Love

BEHIND THE SCENES

(each book can be read as a standalone)

Eras of Us

Not My Fault

Bad at Love

EVERGREEN VALLEY

(each book can be read as a standalone)

Tangled Up In You

How the B*tch Stole Christmas

SAPPHIRE FALLS

(each book can be read as a standalone)

Sweater Weather

THE HOLIDAYS WITH YOU

(each book can be read as a standalone)

I Saw Mommy Kissing the Nanny

Lucky to be Yours

The Only Reason

Ugly Sweater Christmas

POETRY

For Always

Holding on to Nothing

Say it Everyday

Midnights in a Mustang

Five More Minutes

When Lust Was Enough

Isolation

All of Me

Lost Moments

Cosmic

Goodbye Lovers

About the Author

Shannon O'Connor is a twenty something, bisexual, self published author of several poetry books and counting. She released her debut contemporary romance novel, *Electric Love* in 2021. O'Connor is continuously working on new poetry projects, book reviews, and more, while also diving into motherhood. When she's not reading or writing she can be found watching Disney movies with her son where they reside in New York. She is currently a full time mom and full time author.
She sometimes writes as S O'Connor for MF romances and as Shannon Renee for Polyam romances.

Heat. Heart. & HEA's.

Check out more work & updates on:
Facebook Group: https://www.facebook.com/groups/ shanssquad

Website: https://shanoconnor.com

facebook.com/AuthorShanOConnor
instagram.com/authorshannonoconnor
bookbub.com/authors/shannon-o-connor
pinterest.com/Shannonoconnor1498
threads.net/@authorshannonoconnor

www.ingramcontent.com/pod-product-compliance
Lightning Source LLC
Chambersburg PA
CBHW070512300726
48975CB00007B/2407